The right of Emma Michaels to be identified as the author of this work has been asserted by him/her in accordance with the Copyright, Designs and Patents Act 1988

No part of this publication may be reproduced, stored in a retrieval system, or transmitted in any form or by any means without the prior written permission of the publisher, nor be otherwise circulated in any form of binding or cover other than that in which it was published and without a similar condition being imposed on the subsequent purchaser.

Cover Design by
Emma Michaels
Edited by
EAL Editing Services
Interior Formatting by
Dreams2media

Copyright© 2016
All rights reserved.

Crushing Hearts and Black Butterfly Publishing
www.chbb.com

Everyone is dying to live in the...

SHADOWS OF THE FOREST

Sometimes the only way to learn to live is to die.

Dedicated to each of you, who by simply turning the page are making my dreams come true.

Thank you.

起死回生

Wake from death and return to life

PREFACE

ometimes I wonder if we go to a world that is entirely our own when we die. A place people can do things they couldn't in life. Where the paralyzed can climb mountains and see the sunset over a city they never knew existed, the starving can eat like kings and the lonely or abandoned are nothing but loved." He stared at the sky and I smiled softly, he was always so poetic.

"That's really beautiful, Cole." I wished he were right. Mom would be free now and our father, who seemed to wish he hadn't existed in the first place, would be nothing.

"I mean it, Lily. Imagine if we went there together. We could find a graveyard like this one where everyone who died came back, libraries full of stories that never end and Mom…"

"Don't wish them back, Cole. They're somewhere better… At least Mom is." I knew he heard how the words turned to gravel in my throat. She was our weakness, before she died and after. We both know we didn't save her. At least Cole saved me.

"I know. But don't you wonder what it would be like if things were different?"

I stared at him long and hard.

My eyelids were heavy, blinking slowly before I swallowed the lump in my throat and forced the words out. "Well, they aren't. Things are how they are. That's that."

"I guess... What would that world be like for you? If you could go there and do anything, or be anyone?" His voice was fragile; he really did want to know. He watched me as though my answer were my deepest secret and I guess in a way, it was, because it was a secret even from me. I couldn't afford dreams– not the kind that could make me fear losing what I had. It would drive me crazy. The idea of hoping I could...

I couldn't be anyone else. I was broken and that was that.

"I don't know. No point in wondering. All I will ever be is me."

"You're wrong. Promise me, you'll meet me there. Tell me we'll walk that world together. Even if we can't have a perfect life here, we can have one there. We can be whatever and whoever we want. Together."

I could tell he needed this. He needed to know this place wasn't the end. I couldn't tell him for sure what happened to Mom and Dad when they died or wish away his pain. But this I could do. This one little promise, even if it was impossible not to break...even if nothing comes after this place. What these few short words would mean to him was precious to me.

I couldn't help myself.

"I promise."

I got up, but I could hear his whisper as I walked away. "...you are so much more than you realize."

He didn't see me cry or know why I wouldn't tell him. I needed him to have the hope I didn't, the dreams so big they seemed impossible. If anyone could do it, it would be him, but me? I don't dream like he does. Cole was always the only thing I believed in.

He was always the one to save me.

Nothing else mattered.

They gave me three simple rules to follow in exchange for saving my brother's life:

1. Do not enter the West Wing
2. Do not go outside after darkness falls
3. There is only one exit; The Gates.

This is what happened when I broke them...

CHAPTER ONE

I never meant to leave him alone, but it takes less than ten seconds to change the future.

A lost map, a stag, and a forest lane altered everything until the old Lily Rodel no longer existed. An instant felt infinite as my body felt an impact so sudden all of my senses waned until they barely worked. There was no escape. Time slowed as it wound in on itself, becoming indecipherable. Clothes drenched in sweat stuck to my skin. The asphalt's cold surface grated against my side like razors. I lay perfectly still as the cold tore through, digging deeper and deeper. When I tried to open my eyes, my hair, tacky with blood, obscured my view.

A strange pull toward somewhere else took hold.

Footsteps crunched over shattered glass, reminding me of the wind chimes hanging from grandmother's porch— a sound both tantalizing and terrifying. A memory from a past long forgotten, twisting into something new. A soft voice pleaded in my ear, so close I could almost smell the subtle scent of grass and musk I'd come to associate with safety. Something mechanical screeched with alarm before the world went silent and darkness lent me bittersweet comfort.

I couldn't tell you how long it had been when I felt as though I were falling in reverse and had to battle the pain again, vertigo overcoming my senses. The noise came back, the once soft voice now panicked made me want to reach out for whoever was screaming, but I felt the pain release and warmth roll over my body. All I could hear was a steady rhythm beating with my heart, like a pulse sending shockwaves through my body as I lay dying.

Thump, thump.

Thump, thump.

Thump, thump.

...

CHAPTER TWO

Abrasive fabric chafed my skin; a texture unmistakably uncomfortable and distantly familiar. I welcomed the lukewarm comfort of the thin blanket covering me. I didn't want to open my eyes, but no one leaves a place like this until they do. My contrary eyelids were harder to move than I expected, either because of my physical state or because I simply didn't want my suspicions confirmed. A hospital, the last place a girl like me ever wants to be.

Great... There goes our apartment money.

I closed my eyes again and wished the incessant heart monitor would stop already. I knew it seemed morbid, the machine only signaling my life pulse, but the noise was so distracting it was making it hard to think. I'd left the house with Cole, my twin, to move somewhere new and finally start a fresh life together, away from our emotionally toxic family and the small town that confined us.

We had been on the road...

My thoughts came to a halt, my instincts telling me not to think further on the subject, but I'd never been one to listen to my instincts when my mind was set on a different path than my heart. I was that girl who would see the tragedy coming and still stand and hope beyond reason that redemption would come. That something would sweep in and change the way the world worked. I continued to try and remember even knowing I didn't want to— even when the feeling in my gut told me that I was approaching memories I would one day wish beyond anything I could forget.

I paused for a moment, I'd felt that way before. The day our parents died and we were left without a legal guardian. No one in our family was willing to take us in. Two twins they already knew were damaged beyond repair. We could never have been the perfect children they once wanted; beautiful, young and carefree souls.

So, it was just the two of us. No home. No family. Small towns don't really understand murder or what to do with the children left behind. The details of our parents' deaths were never publicly revealed. It was enough to spur the largest rumor mill our decidedly unremarkable town of Silverglen had ever seen. All the good intentions in the world couldn't compensate for good ol' small town fear.

We were finally leaving when...

Where is Cole? I started to panic and my thoughts raced, the screeching machine started to blare faster and faster. I could remember his face. He was lying down, but I wasn't sure where. The longer I focused on my memory the clearer it became.

We were both sprawled out on some sort of faded asphalt. We were getting drenched by cold water that wouldn't stop falling. It took me a moment to realize it was rain and not some strange form of torture. His face looked different. He was gasping and coughing. I reached toward him, desperate to help him and his hand reached for mine, but we were too far apart by so small a chasm it made me ache. It was cruel, being so close, but unable to touch.

Our fingertips barely missed each other's and dripped with blood that was rolling off of us in the rain, as though the world were crying with me as I stared at my brother's broken body knowing mine was too shattered to help him, hearing him whisper words I couldn't quite understand. The blood mixing with the water and spreading a light red tint across the asphalt around us like crimson ink, changing the semi-dark gray to black.

"Calm down, you are going to hurt yourself." A nurse stood over me, holding me down with a firm forearm against my collarbone. The girl in the uniform couldn't possibly be a nurse. I wasn't even sure the girl was my age and I was barely seventeen. She did seem to fit though, like this place was somewhere she spent a lot of time. She might know...

"Where is Cole? My brother..." I continued to panic and the girl nodded in understanding, sitting on the edge of the bed calmly before speaking.

"He is nearby; he just needs more time than you to heal. He is alive and his body is working hard."

I breathed a sigh of relief and lay back again. My body heavy and lethargic. "Thank God." I meant it. I'd believe in God if it meant keeping Cole here, I'd believe in whatever I had to.

"He is okay... he is alive." I heard myself say under my breath as my eyes closed again.

The girl had something in her hands, something attached to the wires and tubes that were surrounding me. Then everything seemed like it was slipping away into the nether. That place between dreams and simple rest where the world was black and you were truly alone. Peace.

CHAPTER THREE

"Time to wake up," a voice broke through the silence as I tried to open my eyes.

They wouldn't yield, even as I painfully tried to force them. I tried to speak, but at first all that came out was a low murmur. It didn't even sound like a noise I could have made. It was too deep and lackluster, like the voice of that guy from our school who always threw footballs at Cole.

"Yeah, we know. It will feel strange, but we need you to wake up now, Lily." They kept speaking, but the fog over my thoughts wouldn't clear.

"Oh, come on. Seriously?"

That time I could identify the voice, the girl from the hospital room. Then I remembered the whole hospital bit with Cole and tried harder to break through the lethargy.

"Do you want to see your brother or not?"

Forcing my eyes open, I welcomed the burning light above me as I struggled to move my arms. Expletives came to mind as pain shot through my side reminding me that my left arm had bandages and might be broken. The words didn't escape, my natural tendency to be quite stifling them. "Ughm... Whaa... FFffffff..."

"Here." The man offered a cup, helping me sit up, he brought it to my lips.

I swallowed and almost immediately wished I hadn't. It wasn't water. Whatever it was, it tasted revolting. I bent forward and started to cough roughly as it made its way down my throat, but when I tried to talk again it was easier and my voice was closer to my own.

"Where's my brother? What happened?" I could see the man a bit better now, he was older, maybe in his forties with short salt and pepper hair. His face was attractive for his age, but his eyes were hard to focus on. The color was odd, almost blue, but too bright and full of life, like the eyes of a child before they understood the world wasn't the beautiful thing they wanted it to be. Maybe they had me on pain meds or something.

"You will get to see him soon," the man said, exchanging an odd look with the girl next to him. "Willow, why don't you go make sure the room is clear so we can move Miss Rodel in there with him."

She nodded and walked off. Her uniform had changed, she wore a skirt instead of pants and while they matched the coloring of the shirts they both wore, I was fairly certain no nurse would walk about in a skirt that short. It looked almost like a tennis skirt, with pleats, but no color. I looked back to the doctor when he spoke.

"My name is Kaede, my daughter found you on the road. There'd been a terrible accident. Before seeing your brother, I need to ask, what do you remember?" His voice was firm and I bit my lip, trying not to remember nearly as hard and I was trying to, my mind turning in on itself. "I know this is hard, but we need to know."

"I don't remember much. I remember being in the road and we could see each other, but we couldn't touch. He was saying something, but I couldn't hear him over the storm. I remember glass, pain, and... a heartbeat. Probably my own, but it was so loud. That's all. I can't remember anything else. Is he alright? He looked so...broken." I bit back a sob. I couldn't cry if I was going to see him, after all, that meant he was okay so there was no reason to. *Right?*

"Okay. That's a good start." The man seemed relieved and smiled, but his voice rang false.

I wished I wasn't so good at spotting lies, but I had seen so many of them, I let it pass. I didn't really care if I wasn't remembering fast enough or something as long as Cole was fine. I needed to see him. Kaede's features were so much more welcoming and calming when he smiled, as though the simple motion could transform his entire face.

"We explained a few rules to your brother, but you weren't awake at the time. We treat any and all patients, many times even free of charge in our clinic, but we ask for them to follow three simple rules. Both you and your brother will need to adhere to them."

He watched me and I tried not to let everything I was thinking show on my face. I knew that hospitals had rules, of course, but his voice had a strangely foreboding timber. I smiled, remembering Cole said I just couldn't trust anything in life might be free after we had eaten a meal at a friend's house. My thoughts strayed to him and I only partially listened as the man continued to speak.

"First, do not enter the West Wing. You can feel free to wander the hospital once you are well enough, but we put very special patients in that wing and no one else is allowed in or out but staff members, for the benefit of their care."

I nodded along.

"Second, do not go outside after dark. We are very close to the forest and have had patients get lost before. This is for your safety, not ours."

"Got it. No wandering into forests."

"And third, the only exit is the set of gates we took you through to get here."

I continued to nod along, thinking to myself that basically it only meant I shouldn't put my nose where it doesn't belong and shouldn't head off into any creepy woods I would probably never want to go near either way.

"Got it," I confirmed and when Kaede looked slightly skeptical I added, "The only place I want to go is to the room my brother is in and I hate forests. My parents died in one. So you only have to tell me once."

The man seemed reassured and smiled again. "Alright, let's get you to your brother then."

The girl, Willow, walked into the room after a few awkward, silent moments and nodded to Kaede, her eyes saying more to him than I could understand. They were hiding something, but I didn't care as long as I got to see Cole.

"Looks like we are good to go," she said directly to me so I smiled, my one good hand fidgeting with the blue blanket that lay across my lap.

"By the way, what happened to my arm?" I asked softly. "Is it broken?"

They both watched me, staying very still.

"Yes," Kaede said abruptly.

Willow looked at him, I couldn't see her eyes from my angle, but her body language confirmed what I already suspected— secrets. I was used to them, I'd always been able to spot them.

"It was injured in the crash. For all intents and purposes, it is in fact broken."

He didn't say anything further as another nurse came into the room and the three of them pushed my bed and the strange monitors attached to me, to a room hardly even two rooms over. Somehow the fact that he had been so close all this time was a comfort— until I saw him. While I had only one arm with a cast, he was covered in them.

I covered my face with my good hand and felt the tears running down my arm. It took me a moment to remember to compose myself— he might be awake. He shouldn't have to worry about me on top of healing, he just needed to get through this.

"Cole?" I said softly, but there was no answer, just a loud beeping that timed with his heart as mine had. I looked up and realized my heart was still being monitored, our hearts were beating in unison. Don't get me wrong, we were twins, we shared a womb, but I don't think any two hearts beat exactly the same, especially when mine felt so broken.

"What is going on here?" I whispered softly, but no one spoke, either they couldn't hear me or they were choosing to ignore me. Again, something I was used to. After my bed was wheeled into place, the nurse left me alone with Kaede and Willow. I refused to care about being ignored, if they were helping Cole heal, then I wasn't going to get in their way, no matter how strange everything felt.

"Has he woken up?" I asked softly and this time they did respond, both starting to speak at the same time, but ultimately Kaede won, the authority in his voice conquering the younger, softer tones of his daughter.

"Yes. He was awake for a while when we brought you here. He is sleeping more often now because it will help his body heal. His injuries were more severe than yours and sleep is the best medicine at this point. The more rest he gets, the faster his body can recuperate."

"Okay..." I didn't know what to think, he didn't seem right. He wasn't my grass stained protector, but someone fragile who had taken his place. As broken by the world as I always felt. I needed to see his eyes, hear his voice. After a while Kaede left, but Willow stayed, sitting in the corner of the room and occasionally checking Cole's stats, chart or just looking at his face for a moment or two as he slept.

I watched the girl, staring absentmindedly. The longer I did, the more unnerving everything felt, seeping in the longer I lay still until it weighed me down, drowsily pulling at my edges. Like something was tugging at my memory, but I couldn't quite grasp it. I finally felt myself lulling to sleep and tried to fight it. But my eyes closed and this time when I fell asleep, I felt dreams coming over me in waves.

I couldn't see anything, but I heard voices, fading in and out of focus.

"You don't understand. You have to save her. I don't care what you do. I'll do anything. Anything! You don't know her. She isn't just my sister. She is so much more than she knows. She is the one who hasn't gotten to truly live yet. I have. I've made my life what it is. Just... Please, just help her."

"Her body is past repair. There is nothing we can do." The voice was hollow and laced with defeat. All I could feel was frost, colder than I'd felt before.

"There is always something, there is always a way. Please, I'm begging you. Please. You can't do this! You can't just let this happen!" Cole. It was Cole. His voice was desperate. "You have to. I'll make you. Somehow I'll make you." His voice lowered to a growl, a side of him I'd never seen before that frightened me.

"Dad, there is one way..." a soft voice broke in.

"It isn't medical. It goes against everything I believe in, don't you understand that? We can't ask him to do that. It isn't natural." Kaede's voice was crazed, a great weight carrying through each word and the strain of it all cracking his voice at the end of his sentences.

"Please, ask me what? Ask me anything... I will do anything!" It was Cole again only it didn't sound like him anymore. It sounded like someone else, someone I didn't recognize. I'd seen him in pain and hurt, but this was different.

"Not you, child. We can't ask Arro..."

I was startled awake, a soft hand pressed against my shoulder. It was Willow, a finger to her lips as she unplugged the heart monitor. "I need to show you something. I need you to understand." She spoke urgently, her voice tender and pleading.

I didn't know what to do, but I wanted the heart monitor to stop blaring so desperately I would have ripped it out myself if I knew how. I nodded to her, I knew the tone in her voice from my own. I wasn't someone used to pleading with others and I could tell she wasn't either. She went to work quickly, and unlike earlier, she was wearing a long white nightgown that nearly dragged across the floor when she moved. She looked different at night with her hair down and her bare feet soft against the vinyl floor. Once the monitors were no longer attached, Willow offered an arm as support and when I stood, I quickly realized why. I wasn't able to stand on my own. Even bending my legs without collapsing hurt tremendously for a moment, but the more I moved the easier the movement became.

She helped me walk to the door and by the time we moved down the hallway, I had gotten my bearings well enough to use the wall for support. "Where are we going?" I whispered to Willow who put a finger to her lips and continued to lead the way. At one point I had to stop, my injured arm was too painful when I tried to swing it naturally and I reminded myself to let it lay still against my side.

The pain made me think back to my dream. I could remember voices, one being desperate and another... Willow stopped in front of a door and motioned for me to come closer. As I approached I was apprehensive, something I knew I should remember was fluttering just at the edge of my memory.

SHADOWS OF THE FOREST

"Follow me," Willow said softly and then turned so that I could see her face and went through the door backwards. I blinked and thought I might be hallucinating as the girl in front of me looked almost like she was changing, darkness crawling through her skin. Her hair turning darker from the light brown it had been, to a black with a nearly blue sheen. Only her eyes did not change, they were still a dark shade of brown like oak wood.

I tried to walk toward her and saw someone come up behind her, a young man about our age who, unlike her, looked completely normal. He grabbed Willow's shoulder and turned her, startling her. She immediately ran and as he walked toward me, I started to feel dizzy. Just walking through the doors had made my head feel like it was spinning, now it was getting hard to focus. He had brown hair that looked red where the light touched it, but as I went to meet his eyes I was suddenly staring at the ceiling. My arm burned ferociously and I could feel myself slowly slipping away from consciousness.

"What were you thinking!" I heard a voice growl even though my eyes were too heavy to open again. My mind was slipping as I heard Willow's soft voice pleading in the distance.

"She can come with us. She can be like us. You made this happen, why won't you let her come to where she rightfully belongs. Father won't even let her say goodbye to him, won't even tell her the truth. At least here she would have something."

"She doesn't belong here. She isn't like us. She belongs in her own world with her own people. She could never be happy here. Just look at what happened to your father and you know what humans did to me. What they have done to so many of us. You know how we end up here."

"You know what I am."

I'd been thrown from the car on collision. I could feel the rain again— covering my eyes, wet slicked hair against my face as the sound of the downpour intensified. My entire body wrapped in pain so intense it made the world surreal. I could see through open eyes that wouldn't close. My entire body refused to move. The water moving my hair in strange patterns around my head, as though someone tried to tuck it behind my ear and the water wanted to push it forward again.

I watched the rain beat down on the red tinted asphalt.

Shoes walked across my path. The further they got from me, the easier it was to tell who they belonged to. I could see my brother's jeans. He knelt on the ground and something else came into view.

At first, I saw something dark moving in front of my vision, then, as it walked toward Cole, I could see orange and white. A fox. As it glided to my brother, it acted as though it'd never met men like my father who would much rather have hurt than helped. Unnervingly innocent, the creature placed its paws on Cole's knees and he leaned toward it.

I could see Cole's face. I'd never seen someone so broken and raw. It didn't even occur to me that he was my brother; the person I'd been closer to than any other soul for as long as I could remember. The brother I'd always known to be an impenetrable force in my life. He sobbed, his breath catching in his throat over and over again. Then, as he leaned down to the fox, he seemed to go still and calm. Fixed in place as the fox turned and walked directly toward me.

The fox looked into my eyes and as I looked back I knew he saw something that changed his expression...if a fox's expression could change.

His tail arched behind him as he came to sit in front of my face. Then, as he moved to my mouth, I felt heat spread through my body as my brother dropped to the ground. He cried out in pain; a cry so guttural that if my heart weren't already shattered, it would have broken. I tried to reach for him and could see him trying to reach for me as he fell to his side, the fox running from us. I cried as I watched someone approach, but I could only see shadows hurrying to carry Cole away before the world faded from view.

A part of him was gone and, somehow, it'd been placed inside of me— I was sure of it.

I woke up gasping for air, remembering the dream vividly. It felt like a memory, too unusual to be fiction and too unmistakably familiar to be a moment that hadn't already belonged to me. I cried out against my better judgment, unable to forget my brother's pain. I didn't need to understand it to feel its effect. I'd seen my pillar of strength crumble. I could feel the fabric back in the hospital again. For a moment I wondered if the hallway incident were a dream. No monitors tracked my vitals and something about the bandages on my arm changed. They held firmer now. I couldn't move my arm from the shoulder down.

I turned to look at Cole, but the thin curtain that once hung against the wall hid him from view. Struggling to get up, I managed to stand and walk to pull it aside. I paused as I stood in front of it, my hand freezing midair as I came up short. The dream ran through my mind like a horse around an oval track, but it kept skipping, repeating the same moment over and over again. The pain coursed through my entire body and Cole...he'd been standing, his left arm cradled against him with no other obvious wounds.

My breath caught in my throat.

Something was wrong with my dream. It couldn't be real, but it was more real than anything else in this strange hospital and more alive than the brother I knew lay just beyond the thin fabric obstructing my view. I raised my hand to my chest and closed my eyes, feeling the throbbing of my heart against my palm. As I focused on it, needing to breathe, I knew.

It wasn't my own.

It didn't belong to me.

It belonged to Cole.

CHAPTER FOUR

I couldn't bring myself to pull away the curtain.

As my fingers brushed the starched fabric I wanted it to be sheer, even though it would defeat the purpose. The sight beyond it would tell me something I wasn't sure I wanted to know. Needing the comfort of the night sky, I left the room. When I was younger, other children hated the dark, but I'd been pulled to it. I loved watching the world change and the glaring reds and oranges of the day turn into soft silver glows and deep blues. When the world everyone else loved went to sleep, my own came alive.

I didn't want to watch a day end; I wanted to watch a night begin. I needed beyond anything to remember that this wasn't an ending. It couldn't be. I would survive it. He was my everything, my savior. I was the one born to die. The one who made my father what he'd become. He was the strength in my life when I had none, my protector. The one stable thing that was meant to outlast me.

I couldn't... I couldn't... I couldn't do it. I just couldn't. There were some people you just shouldn't have to live without. Parents shouldn't bury their children, twins should bury their other halves, no one who shared the experience of a womb should go without the other. This couldn't be happening. I wouldn't live in a world where it could.

Walking down the hallway, I wished the lights weren't so bright.

Hospitals always kept their lights on. I'd learned that much from previous visits. Some things always remained the same. I wished for a moment I had something other than the itchy paper gown as coverage. As I walked, I traced my good hand along the textured walls absentmindedly. Needing to feel something against my fingers as I contemplated memories that couldn't be real. Figments of my imagination that had decided to change what I knew to be true. And somehow succeeded.

Finding a window, I breathed a sigh of relief as I looked at the moon. The sky was clear and cloudless, leaving the stars to shine as brightly as they wanted. I needed a better view. The lights from the hospital shone behind me, reflecting against the glass.

I walked through the halls, trying to find a door to the outside and remembering the times Cole and I'd lay in the grass at night before our parents died. The easiest way to stay away from Father and the ruckus only I seemed able to cause. Anger resonated in the air whenever I'd been in the same room as him. Although Cole and I seemed identical, something separated us, making me the 'bad' and him the 'good'. Our father wasn't wrong about Cole being good, but I didn't start out bad or cold. I became that way, just like he wanted. A self-fulfilling prophecy of sorts—he treated me like I would misbehave so I started to. Not that I needed to do anything to set him off. I could've been a saint and he wouldn't have noticed.

No, Cole was the saint, my hero. The one who deserved to live.

I could still hear his voice ringing in my mind from a night he'd risen to my defense. I'd gone into the yard and laid in the cold wet grass. Instead of scolding me, he'd joined me, facing me. His position so similar to mine I felt I looked in a mirror. His eyes, nose, and lips, everything about us that made us, us on the outside. But it couldn't change the inside.

His black eye mirrored my bruised heart as I told him, "You don't have to protect me. I can take it."

"I know you can," he'd whispered and closed his eyes.

I whispered in his ear softly, "If I could, I'd save you."

I couldn't help but remember the girls who pitied us when our parents died, the novelty of my mourning brother rendering him temporarily appealing. As much as I missed my mother, some secret part of me remained happy father died— even if brutally. It might make me a horrible human being, but we were finally safely out of his reach. For the first time in our lives he was too far away to hurt us again. He could only hurt me through the words that lingered longer than any physical wound— a small part of me believing him. The truth of the matter was; when our family turned us away, we knew they would. They'd never stopped the bad, so why start caring when the 'problem' resolved itself.

We found our chance to escape the small-minded people who believed so little of us. We'd been on our way to the city, where we hoped to find work or even a school— locations no one would know our story. We craved a blank slate– to create futures full of unknown adventure. Now, I couldn't tell memories from imaginings when my dreams felt so decidedly real. I found an exit sign and decided my mind played tricks on me again.

The night air would give me clarity.

Everything was granted equality in the darkness.

I tried to think back to the doctor's rules. "No west wing. No forests. If I wanna head for the hills then look for some gates," I reminded myself pushing the lever and walking into the darkness beyond.

The farther from the hospital, the better I felt. The world around me was familiar again as my eyes adjusted and stars cast their charming glow. I bent down to brush my fingers through the grass. The startlingly cold blades helped my thoughts break through their barriers. I removed the hospital slippers. I felt free and the world around me was beautiful and strange all at once. The stars so bright I stared at the sky for a moment, just taking in the majesty.

My thoughts still vied for my attention. As soon as one would finally release me from its grasp, I'd feel another come over me in a wave. Each new thought making me second guess something I'd already chosen not to believe. I knelt, although I knew better– I could get a cold, but what better place than a hospital? Some part of me simply could summon the energy to care. My brother wasn't waking up anytime soon, and I needed this to clear my thoughts. I was the guardian as he slept.

I needed to steel myself from letting my mind panic over everything from Cole's state to the bill at the end of this long haul. There was no way we could pay it. Not with the meager amount we'd saved for a month's rent at what would likely be a dump of an apartment building. Lying back in the grass staring at the sky, I barely remembered to keep my bandaged arm over my chest away from the moisture.

For a while I just let myself breathe, cold sinking into my bones.

The stars made the rest of the world disappear. Another memory came to mind: the first time Cole found a bruise on my cheek and snuck me outside. The grass, wet with dew, had been such a welcome relief so many nights since. Back then, the chill cut through the pain and numbed my wounds. Now it couldn't touch the part of me that hurt most.

I froze.

Something was watching me.

I didn't know how, but I always knew; A result of years living with my father, trying to stay out of his way. Slowly, I scanned the horizon, at first seeing nothing until I propped myself up on my good arm and switched around. Behind me stood a fox. I stayed perfectly still. I didn't want to frighten the creature away. It was strange to see something so wild and untouched by humanity up close. Some part of me sat enraptured by the sight, unable to force myself to move even if I had the mind to.

My eyes wandered to the bright animal, surprised to see it staring back; standing perfectly still in the moonlight. Its fur shining brighter in the moon's soft rays than anything else around us.

"You were in my dream," I whispered and the fox flinched. Sending its tail whipping from side to side as it slowly backed away.

"You saved me, but you didn't know... You see, I didn't want to be saved. He is worth more than I am. Always has been. I have no place in this world...no place anywhere." My whispers tore from me, as I realized the truth. My survival condemned Cole to an unfinished life. I didn't mind living a life never truly lived, ending before it had a chance to truly begin. I'd accepted the possibility a long time ago.

But, Cole...well, he deserved better. He deserved everything life had to offer from the white picket fences to a loving wife as loyal as our mother. Of course, Cole would earn that loyalty with the sweetest of whispers and the kindest of touches. He would never lay a hand on her in anger and she would feel true love at its finest. The same love that I'd always wanted so desperately.

"Please, can you undo it? Can you save him? I... No! Please don't go..."

The fox started to run. Desperate to believe there might be a way to make a trade, I gave chase.

"Please!" I cried, but the small creature only ran faster. My arm shook with impact each time my foot stamped down in the grass.

"Arro!" I screamed, remembering the name from my first dream. The name I'd almost forgotten. As I ran through the yard, bridging the distance between myself and the fox, I got my first good look at the building that housed the hospital.

It didn't look like any hospital I'd seen before, let alone any building. Beautiful and haunting, it looked like a building straight out of a Victorian painting had been overcome by the wild. Spiraling towers, but modern windows, each lit from within. Except those toward the west which seemed dimmer somehow. The moonlight reflected off the building, showing it had rained recently and revealing a large Red Cross where stained glass may lay if this building had been a cathedral.

Forest engulfed a quarter of the building, vines crawling toward the sky along its walls. Trees so close it looked as if nature itself wished to devour it. I wasn't sure the west wing was safe under so much foliage. I came closer to the edge of the forest, following the fox as closely as I managed and heard running water. A stream cut through the dark green ground. An opening under the hospital with a bridge allowing passage across.

The fox made it halfway across the bridge when I fell at the entrance.

"Stop!" I cried, but the fox continued and as it passed the threshold my heart stopped.

In the blink of an eye, what stood in front of me was no fox. But a man. The one from the hospital doors I hadn't wanted to believe was real.

"Please, save him!" I cried, desperate and terrified all at once.

He disappeared into the trees and I cried out again, losing hope.

Something told me not to cross the bridge, and I remembered the warning I'd been given. Now, seeing the creature's transformation with my own eyes I was more terrified of forests than ever.

No matter what may roam through the trees, it would spell danger.

It always did.

At my core, I'd already learned my lesson about forests. They were no place for humans. I lay there; wishing I could make myself move even though my eyes wouldn't leave forest's edge. I needed to follow him, but my body wouldn't comply. My mind rebelled against the very thought. I hated myself, my body unmoving.

The forest is a killer. Don't do it. You won't survive it. They didn't.

The most dangerous man I'd ever known went into a forest and didn't come out alive. Somehow, the less logical part of my mind imagined him standing just past the trees, watching me, waiting for me. I couldn't escape him in life and I wouldn't let myself die only to fall into his trap again. Terror shook me at my core and I broke, my nails digging into the wood, strange and foreign under my fingers even as splinters cut into the bud of each fingertip. My body wanted to pull me forward, but my fear...

He died. She died. Everyone who entered a forest died.

But wouldn't I die for Cole?

Yes.

Then why couldn't I move?

I felt the tears, hectic and warm, spilling out of me faster and faster until I could only see blurred shapes and colors. A feeling as though the forest were reaching out crawled through me and I reeled back. I couldn't go there. I just couldn't. My hands loosened their grip and I rolled onto my back, needing to focus on my ever loyal sky. Through my tears I only saw dark, and the harder the panic gripped, the less I knew how to fight it.

I hated myself more by the moment, but it was nothing new. I was the weak one. I'd just proven it again. Cole would've crossed it in a heartbeat no matter how scared. It didn't matter. He'd do anything to do what he viewed as right. Then there was me. Lying on a bridge crying over some damn trees that blocked me from the only thing that could save the one person I loved.

I was nothing; just as I'd always been. It was too late, the fox had gone. I screamed, my voice raw and tortured by my own cowardice. I couldn't live. I couldn't be the one to go on when I couldn't even cross a bridge to save a life. It was all wrong.

I just wanted to be human. To be stronger. To not be, whatever I saw myself as.

Nothing.

I screamed and screamed and screamed until even my voice took the route of the coward and silenced itself. I fell into the darkness, wishing I'd never have to leave it again, for it understood who I was, but always accepted me. As with my fear, I only continued to fall into myself, wishing beyond anything I understood how nothing could feel so completely and utterly endless on the inside.

CHAPTER FIVE

My legs felt like frost spread under my skin, frozen even as layers of blankets covered them. I started to panic. The sensation brought me back to the one time I'd been so sure Cole would die—I'd panicked and taken him to a hospital, though I'd driven a few counties away just in case, at his urging. He hadn't let me stop. As much as I'd wanted to risk it, he'd been petrified. The situation wasn't new, but we still didn't want our father to get in trouble. We would be taken away from Mom.

Mom...

The first time Cole had struck back. I'd read once that abusers either backed down like cowards or went into a rage. My father had done the latter.

Cole's voice echoed in my mind, "We can't get him in trouble. He didn't mean it. You know he didn't."

Only I had known he'd meant it. He'd always meant it.

"I don't want to be sent away... You know they'll split us up, right? They won't care that we're twins. It won't matter to them like it does to us."

His voice, genuine and desperate, had made the choice for me, though it had taken us more time to get out of the county than I'd wanted. The entire way I hadn't let him stop talking, terrified he'd had a brain injury. His continued protectiveness over our father had only made my suspicions feel justified. I'd been losing patience faster than he had, but I'd never been the patient one.

"I should've hit him. I should've killed him," I'd growled.

As we'd gotten close to the hospital, I'd known I'd had to keep it together a little longer, to hold off the tears long enough to see us through and continue driving safely. Nothing else had mattered.

"If you'd tried then you'd be the one in this seat and I in yours, or worse, in a cell," he'd said sharply.

I'd wanted to argue, but he wasn't wrong. Our similarities alone had given us proof. If he hadn't been able to beat him, and he worked out, while I ate everything I could ever get my hand on, there'd be no way I could. My sudden ineptitude had hit me hard, almost as hard as my fear for Cole. It'd meant this could happen again and there would be nothing we could do. It'd meant my father had the power, and even together, our hearts made us weak.

I'd wanted to end him so he could never hurt Cole again. But I'd known...in the way a person never admitted until after the fact, the reason we couldn't beat him was the same reason we weren't like him. We hadn't been willing to hurt him. Not the way he'd hurt us. I just... couldn't. And for a moment, I'd hated myself more than I would ever hate him.

He'd hurt people and I couldn't stop him.

I shook my head, trying to force the memory away. Struggling to force my eyes open and my abdomen to lift me so I could sit upright.

"Gruuugggrth." I tried to speak, but my voice broke. I couldn't remember coming back inside. ...I hadn't wanted to. I wanted to lay there and let the world finally have its way and consume me whole in a fit of greed. Even as I wanted the courage to cross the bridge and follow the stranger who might help me make up for his mistake.

They'd saved the wrong twin; both children at the very beginning of our lives just waiting to truly exist. If only one could live, it should've been obvious to everyone that it would be him. He could help people, he wanted so much out of life. When all I'd ever wanted was a chance to truly live— even if just for a moment —and I wasn't even sure what that meant anymore. I finally managed to open my eyes enough to see and struggled to move. Layer after layer of blankets covered me, each one carefully tucked in, in a way that made it harder for me to untangle myself.

I needed to see Cole and know if there'd been any change.

Although attached to the monitors I remembered how the girl, Willow, undid the first few. I took a guess that the others might be noiseless and of no consequence if I removed them. Being careful to turn off the heart monitor first, a simple press of a button, I started taking off cords wrapped around me when I noticed a needle in my arm. I painstakingly slid it out and grabbed a tissue from the bedside to press against my arm, but my cast wouldn't cooperate. Taking one of the blankets from the bed I wrapped it around myself and left the room.

I needed to see Cole, to know he remained alive.

Why did they switched my room?

"Stop right there," someone ordered as I entered the hallway. I stood still and turned slowly. I came face to face with Willow, who looked at me differently now, sadness clouded her eyes.

"Please, let me see him," I whispered to her, but it came out a whimper.

The girl took a deep breath. I feared she wouldn't let me anywhere near him. Slowly she closed her eyes then nodded, determined. "Okay."

"Thank you." I could feel the relief swell in my voice and didn't bother to hide the sentiment from my face.

Willow reached a hand toward me and I took it, letting the blanket fall and following her through the hallways, moving quickly.

"My father is doing rounds in forty-five minutes. If we're quick, we can be back by then without him noticing." She froze as a woman stepped out of a doorway.

I nearly knocked into her before I noticed.

"Willow!" The woman's voice held rage, but Willow stood up to her, standing in front of me.

"She deserves to see him. She didn't have a say in this. Step aside," Willow's voice changed, the softness fading, a sense of command replacing it. It took me a moment to realize she was defending me and my rights.

"I don't care," the woman said, her voice and expression unchanged.

"You don't belong here, you soulless..."

Kaede walked through the doorway down the hall and held up a hand, cutting Willow's sentence off midway. "Stop it. All of you. He took a turn for the worse." The doctor stood there, calculating.

My heart dropped away. My swollen eyes were no longer able to cry.

His hand came to his chin, a finger rubbing back and forth over a section of bristles that seemed thinner than the rest of his two o'clock shadow.

"Please..." I walked directly to Kaede and looked him in the eyes. "... Please. He's all I've got and I'm all he has. We need each other."

"Having her with him might help for a short while," a disembodied voice said from behind the doors. As I cast a glance through the window, my eyes went wide, shock overcoming my other senses. The 'fox man'.

"But not on this side. Not here." His voice turned from strangely melodic tones to gravel with his last words.

I bowed my head and backed away.

"Very well…" Kaede whispered.

"We're losing him." I heard whispered softly from beyond the barrier and wondered if only I could hear him. I knew I wasn't when I looked at the others.

"Can…" I stuttered, unsure if I wanted to voice my thoughts, "Can Arro undo this? Can we trade back?"

Kaede stared at me in horror and the room went completely silent.

For a moment no one spoke. Finally, Kaede closed his eyes and clenched his jaw.

Willow, the first to say anything, spoke softly. "I'm sorry, We… He…"

I had my answer. I remembered what she'd said in the hallway before, about Cole being brain dead, already gone.

Maybe I hadn't done this… Maybe they'd done this. They'd killed him.

It was their fault. If it weren't for them, Cole would be alive and I'd be gone. Some part of me argued that I didn't want to be go. I didn't want to pay that terribly steep price– too steep a price – but I didn't care. Before anyone could move to stop me, I ran at the doors. Needing to find Arro, needing to hear it from his own lips. They'd argued over my dying body. I needed to know what they weren't telling me. I heard chaos behind me, but kept moving.

I barely paused for breath when I crossed, not because of the pain crawling up the side of my bad arm, but because the world through these doors was completely different. This couldn't be a hospital– something so unfamiliar I had no words to describe it. Rather than try, I ran all the faster knowing Cole needed me, knowing that this place held the unknown. It stood for everything I didn't know or understand, all the lies and tricks. We needed to get out.

The lights moved. Floating spirits whipping through the air and as each saw me they frenzied in panic. A stag stood in a hallway and I sped ahead, even more afraid of a beast I knew belonged in a forest. The floors were wooden, with dirt in areas that didn't make sense, vines crawling up walls. Strange looking creatures at every turn. I wasn't sure if I was hallucinating, because nothing I was seeing was possible. A woman made of water, a dog so short his belly dragged along the ground, but tall widespread wings sprouted from his back.

I turned a corner, guessing the way in my panic, tripped and cried out. I looked back to see what caused the fall, but it was only a vine, nothing injured. Then I looked ahead seeing a small body on the floor, hands clasped over its ears, its mouth open as though to scream. The size frightened me. The perfect proportions and dark black eyes against pale skin frightened me more, causing my eyes to widen in horror, but the creature's eyes mirrored mine. As I got up, she did too, as I cried, tears left her eyes. When she screamed, the sheer horror caused me to turn and run the other way, praying I would find Cole's room.

I placed my hand over my heart and pled with it to lead me to him. When I opened a door, a firm hand wrapped around my bad arm, making me cry out as I suddenly whipped around to see the person who held me captive.

"You don't get to touch me!" I screamed at Arro, hurt spread across his features. "You did this to him."

"I..." he started, but when he looked at me he stopped, backing away. As much as I knew I should feel something other than victory, I couldn't help it. I'd found Cole again, and the man responsible for all of this tragedy walked away. Turning to see Cole, I froze, realizing the rage wasn't going away. It wasn't just the pact, it was everything. It was Cole. Why had he thought he could make this trade without me?

How could he not have known?

"Why did you think this was okay? Why did you think you could leave me alone here when I'd have traded anything for you, even my life? Why..." I broke down, unable to move any closer to him. I knelt on the floor trying desperately to catch my breath as pain swept over me. My arm hardly compared to the pain in my chest as I realized this was no one's fault but Cole's, and then realized...maybe I shared the blame. None of this would've happened if I hadn't been hurt. He wouldn't be lying here and I wouldn't be wishing beyond anything that pacts didn't exist and foxes were simply...foxes.

"I didn't want to? It wasn't his to choose," I heard Arro whisper from the doorway and I startled, surprised he returned.

"He's always been my protector. I know he'd find a way, and if he couldn't...it would've destroyed him. I'd have destroyed him. But, this...I can't... Please, isn't there any way?" I begged, not turning to meet his gaze, but knowing he'd heard. He shifted his weight behind me just like the fox the night before.

"The spirit in the hallway– you hurt her. You don't understand she is very sick. You can't do whatever you please here. We aren't like you." His voice was a strange mix of kind and angry.

I didn't care. I just needed to know if Cole stood a chance.

"Please, answer my question."

"Not to my knowledge..." His voice came slowly, giving me a brief moment of hope.

"Your knowledge..." I whispered. My voice trailing off.

"Yes," he confirmed, not explaining, but not dissuading either.

"Is there someone who can help him? Undo it somehow? I'll do anything. Truly...I will do anything. I'm sorry I hurt something... I..." My breath kept coming in sharp sprints, too quick, not long enough to sustain me fully.

I could feel him hesitate, a stillness in the air. It took a moment to realize I'd repeated the words my brother used when he made the pact. I'd do anything. For an instant I wondered if he would be standing here if our places were reversed. If this were just our fate and only one of us could survive this life intact because we each shared some part of the same soul.

"I wish I knew. Ask after Willow's mother. But promise me you won't leave this hospital alone. I am not in denial as Kaede is. Nor do I wish any of this on you as Willow does. I know we can't stop you. At least if you leave this hospital, take someone with you, someone who knows this place. It's nothing like your world with all of its laws and rules. It is wild lands and nothing is what it appears to be. We're all spirits here and you won't understand when you cause damage, let alone how much. Even just getting to this room you hurt a spirit who will now need Kaede's treatment, which only takes away from the time he has to spend on your... Cole. She was someone, not something."

Getting to my feet, I took a step toward Cole before turning back to look at Arro. We watched one another for a moment. Something kept us that way longer than either of us intended. Finally, I nodded, and he returned the favor. Feeling drained, I went to sit on the bed near Cole, watching what little of him I could see through the bandages and wishing I knew how to fix what I'd broken instead of breaking more. I'd caused this and hurt someone else too. I was the reason he was being kept alive by machines and my potential body count was rising.

If I couldn't help him, I may as well have been killed. How could anyone live knowing their life had been paid for by the life of the person they loved most?

The only person who had ever believed in me...

Without him who was I? Someone who hurt others without even meaning to...

Somehow who I was without him made me fear myself more than my father.

CHAPTER SIX

Kaede opened the door, startling me awake. I'd slept upright in the chair again and my back ached. "We can bring a bed in you know."

"I'm fine. Though I am surprised you came back. Did I really hurt some...one?" My voice felt clipped and defensive, making me resent myself more. Even falling asleep felt like a betrayal as time counted down. I'd even been caught in the act.

"You didn't mean to. I'm treating her now and she should be fine. I'm just here to check his vitals. We should have an easier time stabilizing him on this side where the line between alive and dead is thinner, but I don't want to keep either of you here for too long. Arro was right, it's a risk. He doesn't want you exposed to it and neither do I."

"I know I messed up, but I'm staying. And if this is the best place for him, then he is too. Teach me what to do or whatever. I don't know. I still don't understand, but I am accepting it if it means getting Cole back. I don't even know how I hurt that creature, but I never intend to hurt anyone, it just kind of happens when someone is around me."

"Lily..." Kaede started, his voice sad. "She physically feels the pain others feel on the inside..." I knew from his eyes that he didn't want to say it, because he knew how I'd feel. He knew I'd feel as though he knew too much, understanding how much pain I was in and knowing it hurt her enough to place her in his care.

For a moment, she was just a human in my mind. "Is she okay?" I asked softly, wanting to cry. No one should feel that pain, at least not mine. I didn't want it or to give it to anyone else.

"I am hopeful. She is resilient and the contact was brief. My daughter would like to apologize. She's worried she might not be welcome and her appearance changes here."

I could tell he cared about his daughter a great deal. Then, as I sat there thinking, I saw my chance. I needed to ask Willow about her mother and we would have privacy for an apology, wouldn't we?

"Okay, but first, what is this place?" My face was a mask so he wouldn't realize I'd speak to his daughter either way. Information was always more available with leverage.

"Perhaps it is my fault. I drew Usagi here when praying to my ancestors. I'm second generation, but my own traditions run deep. It isn't just Japanese though of course, each spirit who lives there brings a bit more of their culture. Who knows, maybe I drew you here too." He went quiet, his eyes narrowed as he watched me.

I knew it was my turn to give information. "My mother was half Japanese, half Hawaiian." Although I didn't like revealing anything about myself, I hoped it might make him continue. Japanese heritage was the only thing we'd had in common.

"Then maybe you have heard the legends."

"None of the legends were ever like this." I was enraptured by the idea despite myself.

"No, it wouldn't be, would it. Perhaps legends are without culture, but ideas from a collective concept. Fears, dreams, hopes, sadness... it's the same no matter where you go. Even when..." He paused, his lips twisted into a grimace as he looked at his hands. His eyes narrowed before he clenched them into fists. "Can Willow come in? I need to see to my patients."

I nodded, but my nostrils flared in agitation. As he left I couldn't speak, my insides shaking over the idea that anyone might feel my internal pain externally. I feared her, a 'spirit' as Kaede called her, but some part of me, feared for her more. Then there was what I'd said, it bothered me that I knew so little about my own surroundings and scared me that it wasn't about to change.

Turning back to Cole, I whispered softly, "I'll find a way. I'll save you this time. I'll find a way not to hurt anyone else by doing it. I won't fail you... It's my turn, you just heal and I can do the rest. "

"Your turn?" I heard Willow whisper curiously as she stepped inside and closed the door behind her.

"Yeah, he was always saving me." The shadows crawling under Willow's skin still unnerved me, but I focused on her eyes, still so very human. I couldn't keep my train of thought. My mind raced with my pulse and fear threatened to turn my gut so I blurted it out, "Willow, who's your mother?"

The girl flinched as though she'd been hit, turning her cheek to the side from the invisible blow. "I...don't like to talk about her. I just wanted to apologize..." Her voice changed almost completely, as though she had gone from a young adult to a child. "I'm sorry we made the pact and manipulated your fate. It was wrong. It wasn't ours to change."

"Then help me. Please. Tell me who your mother is. I need to know. I need... help." I couldn't remember asking for help before. If I could see this woman I could make a new trade.

"You don't understand," Willow said softly.

"Of course, I don't! That's because you aren't telling me anything.

No one is! How can I understand something without knowing anything about it?" I rambled, frustrated. I needed a plan of action. I needed a solution to help me cope with the fact that I barely hurt and yet my brother's entire body had been covered in injuries he couldn't fight against. "Please, if he's taken a turn for the worse, then I don't know how much time I've got. I need to know. Arro said she might be able to help."

"He told you that?" Her voice was hollow, her normal exuberance drained.

I saw the beginning of the strange transformation I'd seen the day she'd tricked me into entering the West Wing. Darkness crawled under Willow's skin and swirled in ways that nearly held me mesmerized.

"Arro is a Kitsune. Don't mistake his truths for your own. He cannot lie, but he is known for misleading those who do not find his favor."

"A Kitsune?"

"A trickster. He is older than he seems. Time passes differently here. He is younger than many spirits, but don't mistake his intentions. He has never been kind toward humans and he will not start now. Humans are the reason he is what he is; the reason he died in his first life."

"I don't understand. What do you mean his first life? Have you died before?"

"No. To become a spirit you must complete a fate worthy of acceptance to a realm, or be the child of a spirit. I may be different, but unlike Arro, I can die a natural death. I can age and leave the spirit world as a human. Something he will never be able to do."

I had to know... "How did he die?"

"A fox killed by a human's bow. That's all I know. The voice of the forest gave him his name as a cruel joke and cursed him so that he would take on the appearance of a human when in the spirit world."

"I don't understand. Doesn't that mean...being a spirit...that's a second chance, isn't it? He didn't get to live the first time around and now he gets to live as he chooses."

"There are limitations when you're a spirit as to just how much living you can do. But, yes, I guess you could look at it that way. Just don't tell him that. It's probably the one thing you could say that would make him hate you more than he already does."

"But Willow..."

She froze at the mention of her name, her skin softening again as the darkness receded.

"Yes?"

"Can she? Can your mother save my brother somehow?"

"I honestly don't know. I hate her. I hate her more than anything in any world." Her skin turned black as the dark shadows rushed back in. "After what she did to my father..."

Before I could question her further, Willow fled to the hallway, her body nearly a silhouette as the light shone through her gossamer skin.

Choking on utter confusion, I lightly slid the tips of my finger against the edges of Cole's bandages. "Cole..."

I knew not to expect a response. Even in a world where my shock had somehow led me to take ghosts and spirits as reality, I had a habit of confiding in him; my twin, always there ready to swoop in and save the day. I'd call his name and he would answer. I'd be hurt and he would tenderly care for my wounds. Now, he simply laid there. Unable to help, unable to live the life I wanted for him. The life he deserved.

I could be the one to save him.

I felt it. The passionate need, locked deep down inside of me. It overcame everything else. I closed my eyes, thinking back to the times he protected me; all of the times he took the beatings I thought I deserved.

I was the one who angered our father, the one he called 'a disappointment', but he was the one who taught me that I could be more and our father had been wrong. Father looked at me so many times and I knew, without a doubt, I'd be beaten if not killed. He never got far enough to do serious damage, because the second Cole saw the evil in our father's eyes, he stood between his fist and my face. At least every time he'd been there.

"I know how cruel this world can be... But I also know it can be kind. How did you fight it? How did you know not to be like him? You are just always so naturally kind. So caring. You changed the world with your words. I'd want to disappear and be the invisible girl, and you would say the simplest thing and I came back, hungering so desperately for life. Why did you trade? Why for me? You have so much you could do. You saved me and I see the way you look at anyone in need, the way you help and heal every person you touch. I don't do that, Cole. I hurt. I damage."

"It's in his nature." I heard the whisper from behind me; I hadn't heard Kaede enter the room again.

"How long have you been there?"

"Does it matter?"

"I suppose not." He already knew I was dying on the inside, the spirit was proof.

"You put Willow in quite a state. Please understand. She is different. She is neither human nor spirit. She doesn't belong anywhere and we did that to her. Our love created and destroyed a child. That's what shadows of the forest are. They are nearly spirits, but not quite. They're not the same as Arro. Please understand. We truly did love each other...I think," He paused, as if having a debate in his own mind. "Yes. I will always believe she loved me. She tore the veil to be with me for three precious years then asked me to join her in the spirit world... but I couldn't. I'm not strong enough to become a spirit. I never completed such a world-changing act as to earn my place among them."

"Can she save my brother?"

"If anyone can, it's her. She knows all the spirits." He visibly blanched, "But there is a price. Arro told me he would go with you. The forest is no place for those like us, and he neither wants to be responsible for your death nor the death of any spirit you might meet in your travels. He feels humans are inherently violent."

"I'd never hurt anyone on purpose. I...don't believe in that." I didn't want to admit that I wasn't capable of it. I hated myself for my inability to do the one thing I somehow seemed to accidentally cause at every turn.

"Just as it's your brother's nature to heal and save, it's most of humanity's nature to hurt and destroy, whether on purpose or by mistake. The spirit world works differently. It only takes one misstep to erase a life, and one wrong word for yours to be at risk. I can already tell you will go with him, but let me warn you: he will hurt you just as surely as you will hurt him. Never forget that a fox is always a fox."

I nodded. "I won't. But never forget who I am saving. What his nature is. He is worth whatever price I'll have to pay, and I will pay it gladly."

CHAPTER SEVEN

Y ou shouldn't go to see that woman." Willow spat the last word as she checked Cole's vitals, but I didn't need to wonder how a girl could come to hate a parent. I already knew. "She wouldn't help us, her own family. What makes you think she would help you?"

I didn't think she would, to be honest, but it didn't mean I would stop trying before I'd found a way. "I need to try. If it was Kaede, what wouldn't you do?" She stayed silent as she continued her work.

"You don't know what you're getting into," she said softly.

"No. But it's Cole."

"Seriously, you're going to...Ugth..." She gave up on her sentence and left the room. When she came back her father was with her. "We shouldn't let her go. It's too dangerous."

"I know." The moment Kaede agreed, I felt my resolve shake, then strengthen.

Fine, me against the world it is.

"I'm sorry, Lily, but I spoke with a number of the spirits. We don't think you should venture through their world. We won't allow it. We can try to send a message for you, if you agree to stay within the boundaries of the hospital."

I knew in that moment that I was in this alone. Time for the show, as always; the mask to appease the blind. "I would really appreciate that."

I made my face show defeat, but a small pleading smile even, as though I couldn't fight my own battles. There was nothing I wouldn't do. "As long as I can find out if she'll help."

"Well..." Kaede said softly before speaking normally, "I'm glad you see our situation. We'll get a message to her. A spirit has agreed to leave tomorrow and explain the situation."

I didn't speak, my mask was good, but I had my limits, so I nodded and he put an arm around his daughter's shoulder.

"See, I told you she'd see reason. The message gets there either way, she doesn't need to go in person. Feel better?"

Willow didn't answer, I saw her look at me over her shoulder as they turned away.

"We have to check on Kell and see how she's doing. I'll need an herbal remedy for her. Something with sage for cleansing and lemongrass..." Their voices quieted as they left down the hallway and I closed my eyes, trying to reign myself in. I needed a plan.

When I opened my eyes I saw Arro in the doorway.

My thoughts raced as we watched each other. *Tricksters spirit, huh? Alright.*

I watched him a moment longer and his normally angry demeanor softened as it had before for me. I didn't know what power I had over him, what made him so normal to me, but I'd use it. I stood without looking back, afraid I might second guess myself.

I stopped two feet from Arro and smiled sweetly.

"You have a choice. You don't want me to go into your world alone? Then come with me. But I'm going now." I stood tall and let my head rise until I met his eyes. I didn't let myself waiver even as I noticed how endless they were, just like I was on the inside. Endless and dark. Without a word, he held his hand toward me, though at first I didn't notice, still looking into his eyes to prove my point. I needed him to see me as fearless.

I took his hand and said forcefully, "Lead."

He did. I didn't let the shock show until he faced forward, leading me down hallway after hallway, pausing at corners to hide as spirits moved from view. We reached an intersection where we were all too visible and I didn't know what would happen. Then he let go of my hand. He put his fingers to his lips and sounded a whistle. One of the lights above us lowered down to him, just at his ear and he smiled.

"Ready Mi?"

She zipped around him and flew back to the ceiling before darting around to others. A strange show of light and movement I couldn't understand, too frenzied for me to see clearly. He put his fingers between his lips again and whistled three times before looking back to me and grabbing my hand.

Then darkness fell.

No hallways could be seen, no directions. He ran and before I could lose track of his hand, I followed. Fear no longer something I allowed. I was going to take my chance and this time, I wouldn't let anything stop me. Not even a damn forest. Not my fool of a father. Not my cowardly heart. None of it.

I didn't care I still wore a hospital gown, Or that this was a long shot. I especially didn't care that I was afraid. Fear was nothing. It was a symptom– a warning, but not a cause. Something to be overcome or ignored when needed. Somehow I'd forgotten, but I wouldn't let myself forget again. I only cared that I knew the trickster leading me had one goal in mind and in knowing it, I knew how to control the barest edge of the situation. If that could lead me to Willow's mother, then it would be enough.

The rest was cannon fodder.

We reached a pair of doors leading outside, back to the yard I'd run across not long ago. The first thing I could make out was Arro's Cheshire grin. I grinned back realizing we'd made it out. A bit of mischief that felt out of place in my heart, but was a welcome change to the fear approaching with each step we took toward the forest. I wondered if Arro saw my breakdown, if this were a cruel joke when I had a suspicion we could've found a way to go to the spirit world through the hospital.

He sprinted fast as we closed in on the bridge and soon after I heard shouting behind us. "Stop! Arro! Don't do this!"

Kaede was winded as he ran after us, but I was a good runner. I'd been running from my truth my entire life. I could outrun an old man. I turned back for a split second, letting my feet and Arro's hand guide me as I saw Kaede and Willow give chase. Then Arro's hand dropped and the sound under my feet changed.

The bridge.

With Kaede fast approaching I didn't think, I just started to cross. He stopped at the edge of the bridge and held his arm out to stop Willow. "Come back, Lily. We can figure this out. We already found a solution."

"I'm sorry, but I can't wait until tomorrow. I can't risk it," I cried, not for empathy toward those who had helped me, but because I knew I was entering a forest and I had no greater fear– other than Cole dying.

"You don't understand." Willow fought to get past Kaede, but he wrapped his arms around her, more terrified of her entering the forest than me.

"I don't need to. I only need to know that this place can save my brother. I'm sorry." As I said the words I turned, upon seeing the forest I closed my eyes, ignored the tears, and ran.

Rules of The Spirit World:

1. Nothing is as it seems.
2. Everything has a spirit.
3. Belongings Are Sacred.
   4. Belief is power.

I believe I will save him.
That's all I need...for now.

CHAPTER EIGHT

As I passed the threshold, my emotions lay too close to the surface. Something inside of me changed, pushing and pulling as though trying to get out. My eyes watered when I opened them, but I couldn't focus enough to see the forest. For a moment it felt like I might be pulled away from this world by some invisible force that almost pulled me from the car in the world I'd been born into. Tears ran down my cheeks as I thought of Cole.

As though the forest were holding my emotions, my body, and my very soul at its entrance, testing my resolve. I didn't know if it was my mind overcoming my fears, or the forest itself and its strange spirits. I only knew I was completely out of my depth and my pain was rising up like oil and water. Threatening to become one large force inside of me set on turning me around. Cole, the part of this crazy universe that made sense when the world contradicted everything I believed; He'd been the strength that physically and emotionally had always matched the strength that flickered in my soul. The light that Father tried so hard to stifle.

I remembered the pain of impact from the very first blow my father dealt. The emotions that rose inside my chest as the young child inside of me died, giving way to someone who realized that people could hurt each other. The fact that people could cause pain had always been there, but some part of me believed in the best in everyone, and only in that moment, had realized someone could decide to hurt, so locked that part of myself away.

He was supposed to protect me...

My emotions rolled over me in waves, sending shivers down my spine as I fell to my knees. Memories of my life that I'd forced away rose to the surface, one after another, telling me to turn back— that hope was impossible. Fighting, I lifted my good hand, pushing it forward and digging my fingers into the dirt, pulling myself toward the spirit world. I'd already crossed the bridge, I only needed a few more feet. Just a few more paces and I would be where I needed to be. I pulled, fighting my way forward.

Then as suddenly as the emotions had been forced upon me, they released and I jostled to my feet, pulled by that same invisible force. Whatever moved me, yanked my hair and a lock gave way, sweeping away from me. I yelped and rubbed the side of my head trying to stay upright when the wind swept past me, making me sway. I opened my eyes and could see clearly again. What I saw only brought more tears to my eyes. Not tears of sadness— tears of overwhelming beauty I couldn't truly comprehend.

There in the midst of it was Arro, watching me in wonder and curiosity, his eyes softer and kinder than I had ever seen them, as though he had seen what I had just gone through and something about it gave him a sense of wonder about me.

"The...forest has...accepted you," he whispered, his eyebrows knitting together.

I could feel myself trembling. The pain of what had happened collapsing in on what I was seeing. Something about all of it felt so stable, so stuck, like a moment ticking away, but each tick was infinite and indefinable. Part of me knew I had only been staring for a moment, but part of me felt like I might be staring at that world in that moment for the rest of my life, that some part of me would stay there, stuck.

The tree that had taken a lock of my hair rustled in a breeze, the noise oddly beautiful like the autumn winds from our backyard back home. Home. Something about calling it Home when nearly everyone who had lived there was dead, no longer made sense. I approached the tree slowly, watching its deep dark tones. The trunk darker than any tree I had seen before and the leaves a vibrant violet. Turning to look at the rest of the surroundings, I tried to puzzle out exactly what I was seeing. The road forward was bridged with trees like the one I was moving to touch lightly, but odd, small, figure-like statues sat every few paces on either side looking like vigilant guardians.

As my hand was about to caress the bark Arro called out. Ignoring him, I moved forward, my palm against the bark fully now and rested the side of my forehead against it. I was startled to feel something wrap around my shoulder and as I looked, it was a branch of the tree, its violet leaves feeling like soft petals against my skin. I let a few more tears fall into its bark before deciding it had been enough, I needed to stop. I couldn't cry for the past when I was here to create a new future for my brother.

"Thank you," I whispered to it and the branch surrounding me released. As I walked away from it and toward Arro, I almost felt sad to leave the strange comfort, but turned for one last look and smiled as petals fell into the breeze, carrying toward me. Reaching a hand out, I caught one and held it to my heart. I kept it in my palm as I followed Arro who had turned his back to me. He turned suddenly where

I hadn't seen an opening. When I followed, I saw an odd building in what looked like a cemetery.

"You aren't what you seem are you? But you are. You are human."

He puzzled, sitting on the ground, waiting for me. This forest smelled of cherry blossoms and honeysuckle. I took a deep breath before asking my own question, letting the sweet scent fill my lungs.

"What happened back there? The feelings, the memories, what was all that?"

He continued to watch me before answering and I couldn't help but blush at the intensity of his gaze. Standing, he walked toward me and peered directly into my eyes, not breaking contact or blinking until after I had. Replicating my actions back at the hospital.

"You act like it might be a bad thing."

"It is a good thing for saving your brother, it gives us more time. But... I am not sure what it means. I have never seen a human accepted here. It was... I don't know." His voice was odd and his eyebrows knitted together again as he passed a grave, sweeping his hands over it. "Not all of us have graves you know, some of us were forgotten."

"You are here. You weren't forgotten. This forest remembers you and will forever."

Arro froze mid-step and I wondered if I had gone too far. Turning he looked at me, his face guarded, but his eyes fragile. He turned away and walked back to the path of violet trees, walking ahead but I heard his soft accusation, "You just don't understand this place. Not yet."

I looked at the strange, small statues we were passing and couldn't keep my memories from school straight. One would seem distinctly Asian, then the next Native American and so on until the world was indecipherable and all of my thoughts were simply of the souls and the reverence paid to them around the world. Everyone missed someone. Curiously I let my fingers brush against one and paused as I realized when I touched it that I heard voices, soft pleading voices asking for forgiveness, giving prayers, thanking, and begging.

One voice stood out above the others, one soft small voice that was so young and so tender that even though I couldn't understand anything other than that she was in pain, I couldn't help but add my own small thoughts for the child. My own internal prayer to whoever was listening that she would be helped and her pain would be lifted from her. That she might have someone like Cole had been to her, a protector who makes them realize what they have gotten to see of life isn't all that there is.

Seeing Arro had continued on, I jogged to catch up, but let my fingers brush against the taller statues as I went, hearing soft words and hoping that whatever they might be asking for, fate might give them. Somehow as I thought about all of the voices, all of the people out there who were wanting and in pain, I realized what it was about this place that touched a part of my heart I didn't understand. I needed this place. I needed it not just because of Cole, but because it was what I had always wanted, the beauty and awe of the world that was always hidden and just out of reach. But I also needed Cole.

As I continued down the path, I said my own prayer in return for each one I heard, asking theirs to be granted or peace to be found in their own ways. As we walked quickly by, I tried to take in everything I could. I paused when one voice felt so broken that it was as though someone had hit me in the chest. I could remember feeling that way once, so broken and shattered. Even now I felt that inside, but wouldn't let myself become the shattered glass my heart was turning into if Cole still had a chance. As long as I had hope, this could all change and he would be safe, I wouldn't let myself break.

"Please, I feel like I am invisible. How can they not see my pain? I am standing right in front of them, but they only see what they want. I don't understand. Am I even real? Is anything? I just can't do this. I just can't." The prayer was pleading and as I felt my eyes watering I leaned down and whispered to the statue.

"Yes, you can. You can do anything. Believe in yourself. You can." A tear fell and trailed down the side of the guardian. I kept my hands firmly grasping its shoulders as I pressed my forehead to it and heard a soft response.

"I can do it. I can survive this. I will survive this..." whispered over and over again like a mantra.

I let go gingerly, then stared at the guardian for a moment, wondering if the girl had heard me or if she had simply found the strength within herself. Turning, I continued to walk after Arro.

We passed cemetery after cemetery with spreads of forest in between. Each looked unusual and different from the next. As though each hidden path away were a portal to an entirely different graveyard from around the world. As I passed another, I paused, forgetting I needed to keep up when staring in wonder at a large stag. Its beautiful antlers rose high with more points than I'd ever imagined possible. The wind rushed through the trees like whispering voices.

For a moment, my fear of the forest renewed itself, but the longer I watched the scene the more I noticed details about the magnificent creature. It didn't seem like Arro— it wasn't a wanderer through this world, but a part of it. Its antlers rose into bright white tips, but along the sides they appeared almost as wood with vibrant violet flowers that reminded me of the trees. His coloring was a light tan until he moved into the sunlight where he shone a bright white. The reflection hurt but I refused to look away– mystified.

The creature bowed, and not knowing how to respond, I bowed in return. When I raised my head again, it was gone and I could hear Arro hurrying toward me.

"Don't leave my side until you go to Usagi," he warned. "Not even for an instant. You don't understand this place. There are rules, rules you don't know and will probably never understand."

"Then tell me. Help me understand."

CHAPTER NINE

Nothing here is as it seems. Just as I'm a fox, anything you see here was once something else. Something unusual enough to have earned their place here. Just when you think you understand a spirit, you will see their true nature and everything will change. This is simply fact. One you will have to face because anything you see that terrifies you may be the thing that can save your life. Like Kell, the spirit you hurt. She heals people emotionally, but it gives her physical injury. You're ignorance hurt her, your fear, when all she wanted to do was help you. Why? Because she took a form you found frightening even though she is one of the kindest of souls. She knew you were going the wrong direction. She didn't want to take your pain, she just wanted to correct your wrong turn."

I didn't speak. I wanted him to continue. If anything he said would help Cole, I'd listen, even to my own failings. I accepted that I'd hurt an innocent and hated myself for it, but accepting it was better than denying her pain, no matter how badly my nature wanted me to defend myself. It didn't matter.

"Everything here has a spirit. You've been walking around in a daze since the accident, but you have no idea what you may already have done. The simplest butterfly here can be an immense spirit yet one brush from your fingers could take it from this world. If that doesn't scare you, then think of this…that tree took a piece of your hair when we came here. That means it knows you and can follow you from this world to the next if it so chooses."

"Will it?" I asked, feeling the petal still in my palm.

"No. That tree is a part of the spirit of this forest. It wouldn't…but other spirits would. Belief is power, and you have it radiating off you in waves. You need to believe you can do this so you do, but it will attract everything here. We can taste it on you just as soon as we're close to you. I've watched you. You may think you have no belief left in the world, but you're wrong. I can feel it even now." He leaned in close, his eyes hard and menacing.

I swallowed and continued to wait for more, playing with the petal, brushing the softest side against the pad of my calloused finger, unused to such extravagant soft textures. Arro looked at it and his eyes widened further. He glared me down, as though the petal were a lie I'd just forced upon him with my motions, his passionate gaze unflinching. I could tell he tried to intimidate me, so I watched back without emotion. I wasn't about to give him the satisfaction. Instead, I reminded myself that the kindness he'd shown in the hospital and his trickster escape that must have been planned for held his true face. He'd helped me, whatever his motives. "Tell me more, what else do I need to know?"

"When you first see a spirit, never react. Your reaction is your greeting. A simple smile is a hello to us, but more than that, it works as an invitation. We work differently than you do, than all humans and where you are simply a flash of light we are rays that continue to beat down upon the grass. Remember that."

"I will. But keep in mind that in total darkness any light can make a difference and I happen to love the dark. I'd rather be a small flash in the night sky," I responded, my head held high as I continued down the path without him. I could hear his soft footsteps behind me, so much quieter than my own.

"You'll see," he said, his voice vindictive.

I moved forward, my mind set on only allowing the idea of failure to frighten me— nothing else. As I neared an opening I noticed the guardians growing larger as they continued toward a bright light at the end of the tunnel the trees created. "Don't touch them," Arro said, his voice clipped, "They aren't like the other ones. The others would push you to change, these would be that change. If you want to trade your life for his you have to have some semblance of a life left."

I had an unmistakable urge to move toward the guardians and softly caress their coarse, stone skin. The farther I walked from them, the more the impulse grew, as though the stones called to me. Whispering sweetly in my ears of secret prayers too important to be left unanswered. I couldn't bring myself to turn away from them, feeling the pull like a cord tied around my heart. The farther I walked from the stone, the more it hurt, restricting what was already so close to being fractured beneath the weight of what I had to accomplish. I let my eyes slide across the stone, taking in every unusually deep crack for something so slender and spider like, the stone's coarse surface pulling me forward just as the tree had until pain shot through my wrist.

"No!" I screeched, pulling away from Arro. "Don't touch me. Don't touch me..." I panicked, backing away from him, and his anger turned to shock. I no longer cared about the stone guardians. I no longer cared about anything except not letting anyone touch me; instinct battling my logic.

Please... Please... my mind fogged and panic set in, my hand moving to my wrist subconsciously. I could feel it, not what he had done with his light touch to stop me, but the pain that I still held inside of me, too close to the surface. The way my skin couldn't stand contact with anyone but Cole unless I knew it was going to happen. Something about Cole had always been different. I never minded if he surprised me…it didn't hurt like this.

"Just like at the hospital…"

"I… I'm sorry." I bowed my head and kept walking, turning my face away from him. We both knew I'd overreacted, but part of me didn't feel that way, part of me remained adamant of the need to ensure that no one ever touched me again. It wasn't that Arro hadn't touched me before, just the fact that I hadn't seen it coming. I'd been so entranced by the statues I couldn't feel anyone walking toward me, and for a moment, hadn't realized it could be Arro. I knew it seemed irrational after the fact, but while it happened, I only felt the instinctive fear that someone might hurt me. I looked up and realized I'd been so lost in thought that I hadn't realized we exited the tunnel. No longer safely nestled between the archways of the trees.

"Hey, you're going to need to keep your head on straight in here, okay? It will be a shock, but we shouldn't do this if you aren't sure you can handle it." His voice was genuine.

I couldn't look him in the eyes.

"I startled. I won't let it happen again." I didn't watch him, but I knew he put two and two together. I could tell he'd figured out I'd been hit before and I didn't want to see pity in his eyes.

"Good," he said, and I could tell he smirked. "I want your opinion on the voice of the forest. Some consider her a queen, others just a shadow…"

"Usagi?" I asked, remembering what Kaede said about shadows.

"Yes. She has her finger on the pulse, so to speak. She has her place because the forest chose her."

Something about the way he said the last three words made me feel as though his words filled the air with static. The small barely noticeable hairs on my arms standing on end. I thought back to the tree, the way it welcomed me. The way the stag had glistened in the light and disappeared so quickly when Arro neared. Had he seen it?

"Hmm." I didn't say anymore.

He led and I followed closely, unnerved by the field in front of me. Wheat brushed against my thighs and everything seemed to have a slight violet tinge to it. Clouds soared through the sky, not the slow, subtle motion I'd been accustomed to, but quickly, like painted strokes from a master's hand. I wanted to stare, but my head bowed instead. I focused on following Arro and keeping alert to my surroundings. We approached another set of trees, but they felt different. There was movement beyond them, our pace double what it had been in the tunnel.

"The sanctum is close; she stayed near the path to Kaede and Willow."

"Does she love him?"

"Yes. I mean... I don't know. She can be cruel and sadistic or act like a petulant child, but when spirits mate it's different. It means more. A kiss can mean everything to us. She had a child with him so...yes, I'd say she loves him, but it's hard to say. She and I can't seem to see eye to eye. She's hated me since before I could remember. She cursed me. She took away the one thing that meant everything to me. I knew I could take human form, but I was a fox...always a fox. I still am."

I didn't know what to say. He once again became the man behind the mask. I liked that his defenses came down around me. It made me feel like one day I could do the same for someone. *Let them see who I am when I have the upper hand.*

Arro kept moving as we neared the trees, but I hesitated— the movement beyond them, a dark shadow gliding one way and then another like an unimaginably large snake. I remembered my fear of forests, the danger that took away the man so much stronger than I. The hope I'd felt only a moment before that someone might see me for who I truly was disappeared completely. I didn't want to be seen.

I stopped.

"Hey, it's okay." Arro held his hand out.

I didn't know what to do. The ache inside of me was so much stronger than the strength trying to rise to greet it. It forced me to face my personal truth, skewed, but mine nonetheless. My view of the world changed. I'd done it before time and time again. That moment when something inside of me would tell me that everything around me was waiting to attack, take advantage, or harm. The darkest voice inside of me, that somehow sounded both like my father's and my own, whispered that nothing was ever safe. It was both the truth and a lie. But I knew the lie so well that it filled me.

I watched Arro's hand. He slowly started to let it drop, but instinctively I reached out. Some core part of me more afraid of losing the opportunity than making more mistakes to add to my never ending list. As soon as we walked immersed among the trees, the sky grew darker, the leaves high above us cutting off the vivid light that spread across the field. I saw the shadow approaching and felt myself go still, fearing its attack. Arro just kept moving confidentially forward and somehow I followed.

As it moved only feet in front of us. I saw it for the first time and held my breath, remembering what Arro taught me about greetings in this world. I wouldn't hear its movements other than a leaf's whisperings and branches snapping as it moved over them. A dragon. A strange sort of sound that could be beautiful if it didn't come from something so terrifyingly legendary. My body told me it was deadly, shaking in a nervous sort of way, but something inside of me said it was not going to harm me unless I enticed it. The sheer size kept me on edge, it rose to at least twice my height, its round full circumference equal on all sides with the exception of massive taloned feet, leading into muscular legs.

As it moved, it looked like one force of power, the way a snake might as it tread, but this beautiful creature could not be compared to something so normal in the human world. The blue green scales that covered its body converged on a face with eyes so large it took every bit of control not to react. Somehow the muscles and forms, the weight of this creature, didn't terrify me as much as those all seeing eyes, so deep and watchful. What if he saw right through me?

It looked at us then moved pass, unbothered by our presence. As soon as it moved on, I let my breath leave me and watched it from afar. At one point, as we continued walking, it came back past us, speeding ahead of us on its way to who knew where.

"She is going to warn Usagi. When we get to the sanctum, I will let you see the voice without me. Her hatred toward me may hinder your chances. I didn't lie when I said I knew it wasn't my place to decide who lived or died. Your brother...he was just so desperate. He loved you in a way I could only ever dream of loving anything."

"He and I are a part of each other. We even shared our birth and something about it stuck with us. We didn't mind being so alike. It only meant neither of us need ever be truly alone. You're right. It wasn't yours to choose, but... I know he would've done anything. He just should've known I'd do the same."

"When he wakes up, he will."

His confidence made me stumble more than the creature. I looked at him, actually looked at him, and he gave me a half smile. I couldn't help but smile back, realizing maybe I did have someone on my team over here. It didn't change how I felt about him, but it did make me realize that maybe I'd been right and he was someone else underneath it all.

"Belief is power here. All you need to do is believe you can do this and let that guide you."

"Thank you," I said and my voice cracked ever so slightly. He didn't seem to notice.

The forest started to thin, light shining brightly through the space between trees until they cleared, suddenly blinding me. I squinted as we got closer to the light and my eyes adjusted. I thought I saw a hand in front of my face for the briefest second, but the moment was fleeting, and when my sight cleared, there was nothing there except the strangest building I'd ever seen on the strangest little floating island.

The first thing I noticed was the central tree, rising up with great violet leaves, roots poking through the ground beneath the giant mass of land that was held nearly motionless over what reminded me of a sinkhole. It went down into darkness for as far as the eye could see, but waterfalls dove down into it from three different section of the outside. Water seemed to pool upwards from the base of the mass, falling sky-ward in a circle around the building, parting at the bridge where even now spirits of all kinds entered.

Arro gave me a moment to stare. There was nothing like this in my world. How could there be? This was not made by the destructive hands of a human, but a phenomenon created by the forest itself. It built a palace for its voice, with layer after layer of Asian style slats coming up into thinner and thinner points as the palace reached for the sky, never for a moment climbing higher than the tree that gave it life. Although the bridge seemed full of color, the palace itself was entirely deep browns and violets of the tree, formed from its very bark.

I continued forward, taken aback by the beauty of the building and the way the sky looked as it might at sunrise— full of pink, violet and orange, but with gold dusted clouds. I watched the spirits crossing the path: a woman made of water, a large cat of some sort who swirled with darkness and had strange glowing blue runes across its fur like spots, and an elephant. I couldn't help but stare at the elephant, trying to riddle out what seemed strange about it. Next to its companions it looked so…out of place, but somehow it, like the stag from earlier, fit the land around it, even more so than the building, which as I watched more intently, seemed to be alive. The longer I looked, the more some part of me, that seemed to be coming out more and more in this world, made me think this palace felt like it belonged to someone, like a cage, not wild and free; and I was trespassing.

"I can't go with you," Arro reiterated.

I hesitantly started walking forward, keeping my eyes open too long, too terrified to blink. Like the world might run from me or attack me at the slightest threat. My good hand fidgeted with the cast covering my other arm, pulling at the edge.

"Are you sure?" I called back to him, hesitant, I'd only walked a few steps into the open space and already could feel his absence.

"Remember what I said. Belief is power."

He met my eyes as he said it and I felt a shiver roll through me again.

Instead of instilling fear, it reminded me why I was here, whose heart beat in my chest, and how desperately he needed it back. I lifted my head, realizing I'd been bowing in fear of being noticed and walked confidently forward. As soon as the light hit me and I'd shown myself, all three creatures crossing watched me, only the elephant stopping with what I would describe as a smile.

I walked by the cat and had to steel my insides so fear didn't get the best of me. As Arro had said, nothing here was as it seemed, and I needed to prove that I could be the same. I wasn't just some girl with nothing to offer. Part of me wavered as it always would, but another part of me rose up to meet it, my body spreading with the warmth of love I'd always felt for my twin— my other half. I knew I could do this. I needed to. The woman made of water turned toward me, but the snobby look wiped from her face when the elephant came to my side and walked with me.

"Child, I will walk you. Where be you goin'?" The elephant's melodic voice obviously hadn't become accustomed to English.

I looked to the trees where I knew Arro waited, but I couldn't see him.

"Needn't worry, child. I Baku. I ze nightmare eater. I protect ze hurt humans. Remember all, childs. You felt pain… You felt hurt. I won't let them hurt you."

I didn't know what to say, I simply did as I had with the tree and lightly touched his side. As though he understood my answer, he once again made the motion I could only describe as a smile.

"'Ere, child," he said, and before my eyes his ears crumbled into sand, his body eroding into nothing but sparkling golden dust which swirled in circles in the wind. My breathing grew harder, terror getting the better of me again until the dust started to reform into a new shape, much like my own. In a moment, he stood before me like a shimmering mirror. "Now I can speak so that you can understand, child," he said in my own voice, but my eye twitched ever so slightly hearing the word "child" slip from my lips.

"Thank…"

"No, child, never thank a spirit," he said quickly, his finger moving to my lips to stop me. He looked around to see if anyone heard and breathed a sigh of relief seeing that the water spirit and the cat had moved on. "Don't thank a spirit; It indebts you to them."

"I need to see Usagi to save my brother."

"This child?" His body shimmered and with the simplest of changes in stature, hair, and facial features he resembled Cole.

I closed my eyes for a moment as they filled with tears I couldn't let fall. "Yes. How…"

"I told you, I eat human nightmares. I remember each one, each person, their pain and the happiness that rises to replace it."

I distrusted his words. I couldn't let him discredit me to Usagi or she might not hear my plea.

"Don't fear, child. I will not betray you. Your pain was given to you, not created by you. I judge not. Follow me." He reached his hand toward me, but I didn't take it. As I started walking forward, he smiled with my lips, my mirror body showing just how much of a toll the car crash and the events following had taken.

I couldn't look at him, couldn't keep watching my own face and thinking of Cole's. How easily my features flickered to his when Baku showed me his face. "Sorry, child," he said, and once again I stood next to an elephant, his trunk rising from between his tusks as he rolled his head toward me when he spoke. "I didn' mean to…" His voice was overcome with sadness.

As he led the way, I wondered if he ate the nightmares because he truly cared. Maybe he felt them instead or something horrible? How did he pass between worlds or did it work as the prayer stones had? I had so many questions and no time for answers. Already I felt the journey was taking too long.

We'd reached the entrance, but I couldn't see guards. Whatever threats she faced in this world I had a feeling she could deal with on her own. The doors stood startlingly large, but open in an almost welcoming manner. As we walked, the halls grew distracting, the wood framed sheets of ever moving water flowing up and through cracks in the ceiling, probably creating all of the walls in the multi-layered Asian styled palace. An image came to mind from a book I had once looked at in my mother's library titled 'The Imperial Palace'. I could imagine the architect turning green with envy if he ever saw this place. It held the regal airs, but the water that rose as its walls flowed crystalline blue.

"Child, be ready," Baku said, and as I looked at him, it put this palace into better perspective. He easily walked through this hall with room for others next to him, almost as though this palace were built for much larger spirits. We approached a hallway with statues on either side, and I watched them, sitting there so unlike the ones from the forest. Then one blinked and I bit my tongue to stop from jumping, remembering again the warnings Arro had given me.

Baku nodded his head toward one of them, then another, but ignored the rest muttering, "She-lions."

We were close. The She-lions must've been Usagi's guards. My thoughts reeled, my mind trying to regain focus and keep me strong, even as I heard haunting chimes in the distance. We approached an extraordinarily large set of closed ornamental doors, even bigger than the first set and I turned to Baku then nodded my head instead of thanking him. After a moment I smiled back at him for the first time, he'd been true to his word, he'd chosen to help me expecting nothing in return.

He bowed his head, mirroring someone new, someone I'd never seen. "Good luck, child. Your brother shall have good dreams."

Warmth spread through my chest, his kindness giving me the strength I needed. "Does he still dream?" I found myself asking even though someone who is brain dead couldn't possibly dream.

"He is dreaming now, child. Dreams of you. Of happiness."

My smile spread as he changed back into his elephant form, and I pressed my hand against his trunk as it coiled to meet me. I turned quickly, when I heard a crack like thunder, and a new set of doors started to swing open.

CHAPTER TEN

They called Usagi the voice, but she walked more like a queen. She faced an opening in the wall and for the first time, and from this height, I could see the sheer scope of her world; breathtaking and more extensive than I'd ever imagined. This place wasn't simply a forest, it was a world of its own.

When Usagi turned, I thought it must kill Kaede every time he looked at Willow. Although Usagi stood showered in grandeur, there underneath it all remained the spitting image of her daughter. Yes, the crimson kimono and vibrantly jeweled headpieces seemed like the most beautiful of distractions, but her face, deep dark locks of perfectly straight hair draping to the floor and the dark ink that swirled around her wrists before plunging her hands into darkness would make the resemblance obvious to anyone who cared to notice.

She floated across the ground so gracefully that my comparison didn't last long. Usagi wasn't like a queen, she moved like a goddess. What had she seen in Kaede? Had he been some great beauty amongst men in his youth or had she grown so tired of her spirits that any man would do? I wanted to ask, but wouldn't dare. Maybe there'd been something about Kaede I hadn't seen, my view too skewed by the situation and the stern man who didn't want me to be here this very moment.

"Were you sent here, child, or did you stumble upon our forest?"

Usagi's voice sounded strange, like accents from a thousand different languages fought as her mouth formed words in a language that obviously felt unnatural to her, though I wondered if her aversion were manifested and not natural. I wanted Arro to appear, but if Usagi hated him, she didn't seem like the kind of beautiful creature I'd want to see angry.

"Kaede sent me." I had no idea why I phrased it that way, but something inside of me told me it would make her listen.

"Leave..."

I thought she spoke to me, but when no one moved she turned to her guards and stared them down. One gave a momentary look of defiance in return until her eyes met his, filling with malice as his filled with fear in exchange. He nodded to the others, bowing his head low as he made his way out. As I watched him go, I couldn't help but shiver every time one of his sharp claws tapped against the wood, imagining them lunging for me if this meeting didn't go as I hoped.

For the first time I truly took a look at the room, not just the beautiful view or the strangely simplistic chair in the center. The wood across the floor was one large piece, the rings in the wood visible.

Pillars held up the roof, but only water flowed toward the ceiling and through the open window to separate her from nearby hallways. It was a wonder I hadn't noticed her while walking, but Baku had been between me and those walls. When the doors didn't close, I was struck by the realization that with water walls she had no privacy. Then the water quickened as it showered toward the ceiling in thundering waves.

"Speak, child...please..." Usagi's voice had changed— younger, less formal and when I watched her face she looked so much more human. The ink around her wrists and hands spreading through her skin as Willow's had. "Please...is he alright? Does he still live?"

"Yes. He is healthy and alive, but my brother..." I choked.

I didn't mean to.

I hadn't even been thinking about Cole until that moment, distracted by her presence and when I did, the emotions swept over me again, hitting me so hard I had to take a second to clear my mind. I needed to remember that this woman could help— the only person who might stand a chance of healing him. "My brother is in his care and dying in my place. A kitsune made a pact when my brother, Willow, and Kaede requested. But I don't want Cole to die for me. I want his life restored."

"You stupid human," she spat, looking away from me.

I feared she realized he had not sent me. I'd run. When she looked back, I couldn't help but stumble, catching myself and standing my ground as she came toward me.

"You don't know the gift you've been given, you rude insolent child. You should accept a gift given so freely."

The terror she sent roaring through me left me speechless, but then I saw ink trail down her cheek like a single tear before disappearing under her elegant kimono.

"No—" I couldn't say anything else for a moment and it caught her off guard enough that she turned back toward me, her anger flaring again, but I couldn't allow myself to back down, no matter who she might be. "I won't let my brother die in my place. We both know life is worth living because of love. He's who I love most in this world. My twin. You are asking me to exist as half of myself and I refuse. He saved me time and time again, and I won't turn my back on him now— the one time he needs me to save him from himself."

She watched me in a way I'd never been watched before. I couldn't put words to it, but after a moment she spoke, "What is done, is done, girl. Take your gift and go. This forest won't..." She trailed off as she stood there watching me.

Her expression changed as though a thought hit her with such intensity she no longer felt present in the room, but far away inside her own mind.

"Usagi? Please, can you help my brother? Can you heal him?"

When I said her name, she turned back toward me as though the sound of the name sent a small thrill through her though I couldn't understand why. I just wanted answers and nothing more. I wanted to leave, but only if I could help Cole.

"I am not sure. I must speak with the heart of the forest then return." She walked toward the door and I jogged to keep up, but needed to ask something. I was a thousand times more hopeful than I'd been a moment before and it spurred me into motion.

"Does that mean there's a chance?"

"It means there is hope." Something about her voice caught me off guard, but I clung to the words desperately. In her hurry, she swept down the hall and I followed closely.

She paused suddenly. "Wait. What kitsune?" She turned toward me her eyes narrowing.

I swallowed hard. My stomach turning sour as her eyes bore into mine. I let my faith in my brother sweep through me, holding me steady. "Does it matter?" I asked.

Her head slowly tilted in thought. "I suppose not. Not if there is hope." Again, the way she said hope sounded odd. Like she didn't mean for Cole, like this seemed all too important to her all of a sudden. "I will warn you, child, but you will owe me a debt of warning in return. The kitsune you speak of is only with you to break his curse. He wishes for only one thing— to regain his fox. Don't let him have it. He doesn't deserve it and he knows it's something only you, or a human like you, can give. A humiliation of a curse that requires him to receive a kiss from what he most despises, the very species that killed him and sent him here. I read something like it in a book during my recent years in your world. It was too good not to try."

I winced, but caught myself and left my face expressionless, not wanting to give an inch to this woman until I could better understand how the situation had changed.

When we turned another corner, Baku was walking away from us.

"Baku," she said.

He turned.

"My friend, will you please protect this child until I return?"

He'd been so kind to me that when he watched her face and his own turned steely, immovable and emotionless, I grew confused. He once again shifted into golden dust then reformed in her mirror image. "My lady. Do not. Enough injustice has been done. Please…"

"BAKU!" she screeched, "if you will protect this child, I will be eternally grateful." Her eyes narrowed, the ink swirling around her wrists crawling to the top half of her face, red flashing across like a lace mask. I remembered Willow having something similar happen and realized it was anger spilling over. Black held emotion, red showed anger, and plain skin most likely inferred a calm state. Her emotions must have literally been eating her up inside.

"Wait. Usagi? Willow…" I started, but she turned to me and her face changed, blue ink crawling quickly up her arms, washing through her. Any doubts I had about her love for her child disappeared.

"Very well, my lady," Baku interrupted, looking at me.

Before I could say anything more, Usagi sped ahead, her mirror made of golden dust still lingering behind.

"Child, I cannot tell you her fears or dreams without permission from the heart of the forest, but I can tell you this: there is nothing she wants more than to be with Willow and Kaede. I am sorry. So very sorry."

"What do you mean? She said she will save my brother."

"Yes, I think she will, child. I think she will…"

I didn't mean to be pig headed, but for part of the conversation with her I'd felt so sure hope was gone and the feeling in the pit of my stomach was still lifting, slowly rising out of me as the hope settled in its place. I couldn't allow myself to lose hope again, after all, belief is power. "Then that's all that matters."

"No, it isn't, child. No…it isn't." Baku reached his hand toward me, and I took it. The dust soft and instantly exhausting. I had no idea how time passed here, only worried I might drop to the ground right here in the middle of the hallway. "You love your brother more than you have ever loved anything, don't you?"

"Yes. He was the only one who ever loved me."

"Your mother…"

"NO," I said, stopping him in his tracks. "Not enough. Not really. She loved me, but she didn't LOVE me."

He stayed silent, but continued to wear Usagi's features like a mask as he walked with me.

"Where are we going?"

"I want to show you something I think you will find very beautiful. You like stars, the moon, the night sky, the darkness. Time is different here, though still unyielding, light and dark are both fleeting. If we get

out there quickly, we can watch the graves crack and the sky crumble."
His voice slowly adjusted, mimicking the tones I'd used earlier.

"What?" Somehow I'd adjusted unusually well to the weirdness of
this place, but his description still sounded strange; too fantastic to be
true. I hadn't told Arro, but I'd always felt an affinity for graveyards.
They felt to me how church might feel to others, not because of the
dead, but because they were peaceful and centering. I never felt alone.
I didn't have to worry about putting on a show for anyone, or trying to
play the mourning daughter, when in reality I hadn't known what to feel
or why I should feel anything at all.

Though my mother...

I always wanted to mourn my mother, but some part of me wouldn't
allow it. I would sit by her grave and talk to her as though she'd been some
other woman, someone I could've been close to. Then I'd look over and
see my father's grave next to hers and the emotions would roll over me,
confusing me beyond understanding. To the point where my questions
would overtake everything else and I'd leave. I'd walk to the gardens lin-
ing the graveyard and pick flowers to set beside the graves throughout
the graveyard that had been left untouched and forgotten, their grass
not even trimmed in years unless they were the recently deceased.

Looking at Baku, I feared how much he knew about me, but I guessed,
with dreams being what they were, maybe he'd earned his knowledge.
Maybe he knew everyone's great fears, regrets, and the things they never
dared tell a living soul. If he did know the worst in people, it made his
feat exceptional that he still wanted to take nightmares away. Give the
good dreams for the bad. I couldn't help but admire him. His size would
normally intimidate if it weren't that he seemed the most normal thing
in this world so far and the kindest of souls I'd met in a long while.

"I have a...friend in the woods."

"Your fox will see us and follow."

I nodded. Out of nowhere, the golden dust version of Usagi once again turned into an elephant. His large form stopped and bowed down, lifting a stump of a leg at an odd angle. I watched, confused, and he nodded his head toward his back. "On. Ze tired child."

"Oh." Walking next to an elephant was one thing, but riding one... I'd never even ridden a horse. Even a rollercoaster wasn't on the agenda with my parent's hermit-like tendencies. I'd never have gone to a fair if it hadn't been for Cole whisking me away to a day full of funnel cake and mirror houses. The rides were too intimidating, the animals were enough for me. Now here I was, being asked to ride an elephant who wasn't really an elephant at all. What once would've been a dream come true. I hesitantly put a hand on his rough leg, comforting like the co-lossuses of my brother's hands the year he decided to learn how to play a guitar he found at a yard sale.

I climbed onto Baku's back and let my legs slide to either side just behind his ears as they lay back against my thighs. He started to walk. For a second I thought I would fall and nearly toppled forward. He chuckled and I steadied myself.

By the time we reached the bridge again, I'd managed to settle down other than occasionally shifting too far to one side. Once I let my body shift naturally with his movements, understanding the rhythm I could settle in, almost as though I were being rocked to sleep. He walked slowly alongside the forest, making his way to the far end of the chasm.

As we passed the forest, Arro joined us. "How'd it go?" he asked, his mask of self-importance once again putting on a show for his 'audience', but Baku didn't seem to pay it any mind.

"She is going to talk to the heart of the forest. She said there's hope." My elation shone through in my voice even as I wobbled atop Baku's back, trying not to fall asleep as we rocked from side to side. I almost didn't notice the look Baku and Arro exchanged, Arro seemed suddenly nervous.

"So what's the price?" he asked.

I shrugged, trying not to let my eyes close. "She didn't tell me and to be perfectly honest, as long as it saves Cole, I'm not sure I care. Baku, how will we know when she's back?"

"I will takkke you back to ze palacccce when you've zeen the gravessss."

"I am so happy to have met you both. So happy that Cole will be okay," I said and my words almost slurred. I was so close to passing out. Baku was right, the sky got darker quickly, pinks and oranges turning into purples and blues, so far without stars as the clouds passed through the sky, flying away from us.

"You should worry about the price, Lily. It's important."

"I just..." my lethargy weighed me down so heavily I couldn't even think straight.

"Oh come on, Baku. Contact with you is only making her worse."

"I am one of the few spirits here who actually likes you, fox, but even I find it strange that you're helping this human. Let her sleep. She is so very tired."

I blinked drowsily and realized he spoke with Arro's voice and stood with me in his arms. Once again a body made of golden dust. I blinked, a bit more alert at the sight of Arro holding me, and struggled out of his grasp, suddenly trusting Baku less.

CHAPTER ELEVEN

What had I done? Arro was right. It dawned on me as I returned to a normal state of lucidness. I'd been so terrified she wouldn't help that when she finally did offer, I took it without a second thought. I didn't know the price or what made her change her mind so suddenly. The thought that dawned on her could easily have been something detrimental to me; something that risked or stole more from me than I could ever expect.

I started to panic and turned to Baku. "What was she thinking? You know. You argued with her over it. What is the price?" My voice held more accusation in it than intended, but it already came out and I couldn't change it.

"Child..." he said softly, almost guiltily.

"No. Don't 'child' me. Give me a straight answer. You claim to know so much about me, but if you do you know I am no child and never was." I felt anger rising, spreading through my body like heat.

"Lily—" Arro tried to come toward me, but I backed away.

My mind translating anyone who might stand between me and my answers as enemy. Baku made me sleepy on purpose and I was sure of it.

"Baku lives by different rules than we do. He must adhere to the rules of the pocket realm he is in. Here, that means the hart of the forest has his secrets and Baku is expected to keep them. I am not saying you shouldn't ask questions. You're asking the right ones. I am saying you need to calm down and think about this all very carefully."

"You don't understand..." I started, but he interrupted.

"Oh really? I'm not the one who was just furious at you for not even asking? Is that what you're saying? I know perfectly well what you are going through or I wouldn't be a damn human in this world thanks to that woman and her prices." He spat the last few words as though they sullied his mouth. His anger made his hands clench at his sides and although they didn't move I saw fists. Even knowing he was only holding his own tempter in and didn't intend to hurt me I couldn't see it. My mind and my instincts trained to be too different; two distinct entities instead of one part of me that might work in tandem.

"I would pay anything, but I need to know... I..." I paused. He'd said I was asking the right questions, but Baku couldn't expose secrets. If he could answer my questions without exposing secrets, I might learn more than foolishly trying to use my words as a form of force I couldn't uphold. "Did Usagi realize something during the conversation that changed her mind?"

"Yezzz."

"Do you know what that something is?" I started to calm down as I better understood what Arro had been telling me.

"I fear so, child, but do not know for certain." He changed into Usagi's image as he continued speaking.

"Is there any part of what you know you're able to tell me?" I asked, using one question to ask many.

"Yes. Her past is a secret, but affects your future. She hopes to make a deal of her own, because what you ask is out of her power, but not out of the power of another." At Baku's words Arro's jaw dropped in an uncharacteristically graceless movement.

"The hart," Arro said, then turned to me. "Whatever it is, she doesn't know the price yet either. At least not for sure. She has to commune with him to discover it."

"I…" My mind couldn't catch up fast enough to track all of the nuances of the situation, but I knew this meant everything was uncertain and I needed to hold on to what hope I did have. Even if it meant possibly sacrificing something else equally as necessary to me. "I am sorry for snapping at you both."

I wanted to thank them for answering my questions, but I was not going to indebt myself to them even if they were the two spirits who might not use it against me.

"We all got here somehow and no one's story is pretty. We don't all see eye to eye, but we understand the power of emotions." Baku stole my form again and I found it hard to look; to see the mirror image of my body and know whose heart lay inside it.

"Maybe I should come with you when she returns," Arro said softly.

"No…"

"Yes." Baku and I spoke at the same time, his yes overpowering my no. His tone serious and the melody that always weaved through it having disappeared. "I don't trust her with this. I don't trust her with you." He changed his appearance into Cole for the last sentence, and I had to turn away.

Anger rose inside of me, and as much as I wanted to unleash it on Baku, I knew it belonged to Cole for having put me in this position, for having left me here. As much as I knew it was selfish, I wanted him to be the one suffering without me because the pain was just too much to bear, the idea that he might not make it or that the price for his life might be too high.

But what price wouldn't I pay?

Was I really so angry at him...or at myself. For the chaos that always seemed to surround and feed off of me that finally swallowed my brother whole. I'd caused this. I wasn't sure how, but I always caused chaos everywhere I walked and I had no right to wish it on him. The clouds began to clear from the sky, and as soon as they disappeared, the stars started to light.

First one or two like lightning bugs, but then strips and layers added, flashes of lightning burning bright and leaving unimaginably beautiful stars in their wake after they disappeared. As I stood before a part of the clearing with short grass, I could feel the ground rumbling beneath my feet as thunder roared. Before my eyes, grave markers spread through the field and rose from the ground.

I'd never thought about how many people died in one day before, but that was the guess that came to mind seeing the vast expanse of graves in so many varying types, shapes, and sizes. Even mausoleums. Slowly, the sky lit with new colors, a vibrant gossamer green ribbon that moved as though it flowed in the wind.

"The aurora. The northern lights, it crosses over sometimes. Have you seen them on your side?" Baku asked.

"No," I answered too softly. I felt breathless, standing riveted in place as I watched the light flickers of pinks and yellows intermingle with the green, the stars shining through. Then I noticed the sound of wind, so strong it nearly howled, pulling me toward the graves.

Graves were disappearing.

"The after-life is accepting them. It's the spirit world's way of paying respect to each soul that passes through the pocket realms, the afterlives like this one or onto whatever comes next." Arro's soft voice made my head tilt forward as I bit my lip. I closed my eyes for the briefest of moments when a shiver shifted down my spine at the warmth of his breath on the back of my neck. I wanted to turn toward him, but I didn't want to miss watching this tribute to the dead. The order in which graves disappeared seemed random from what I could tell, but as I looked closer each grave had one small fleck of light that released from it and rose into the sky like a star, painting the sky grave by grave, soul by soul.

Maybe this world accepted me because I wasn't meant to live.

Standing there, the sky got brighter even as the ribbon of light started to fade. "It's wondrous." The idea that even if Cole lived he would never see this, made me want to curse whatever force had chosen our fates. Instead, I whispered tenderly, "Why?"

"Why what?" Arro asked, his voice curious but confused.

"He will never see this. Even if he lives, this place is so unbelievable. He would love it. I was the one who couldn't believe in this kind of stuff, he was the one who thought that anything was possible, that the world was full of unexpected beauty, and life was the most beautiful gift anyone could be given. He was the one who should have lived, but even if he had, this place... I wish he could see it."

A hand gently wiped away a tear I hadn't noticed against my numb skin. It finally sank in that although there might have been hope, that hope was all I hung on to, like a thread holding me from falling off the edge of a cliff. I could feel it, the way my heart teetered, ready to shatter as my body had in the accident. On my other side a hand grasped mine, and when I moved over Baku was a golden dust image of Cole.

I broke.

I couldn't help it.

I squeezed his hand, pretending it was Cole so hard that some desperate part of me believed it, that he could see what I saw— the incredible majesty he'd always told me existed, but I'd never believed. Something about it changed me, not making me any less the girl he'd known, but making me more... me in a way I will never know how to describe.

Arro softly took my other hand, but as I watched the sky, I could feel him watching me. Something about him seeing me this vulnerable terrified me because it felt so freeing. I had never let anyone but Cole see me and here I stood in another world and emotionally transparent to two people who already knew more about me than anyone other than the one person I fought to save. The person who'd brought us together.

Somehow standing there and letting my heart fool me into thinking that Baku truly was Cole made me wonder if I could be that girl. The one Cole wanted me to be, who could believe in absolutely anything, especially in the good. The girl I'd tried so desperately not to be for so long. For just a moment I let myself be her, let myself feel like she would, let my eyes follow the green ribbon with wonder and forget that the world crumbled inside of me just as the graves in front of me who turned into the stars that illuminate the night sky.

It was everything.

All of the emotions... just everything.

As the last grave burst into a brilliant bright light only a few feet in front of us, it rose into the sky and broke through the green ribbon. The sky flashed white, blinding me and bringing me back to my senses.

I didn't want to come back.

I didn't want to stop being her, for a split second, before I remembered who I was and how I'd become what I was. Before I remembered that my father wasn't the only man I'd learned to hate. I'd seen the worst in people the world saw as saints— when they saw me as so little and I wanted everything so badly. I just wanted good. I just wanted love, but I'd seen the different types of love and truth in love was rare.

"Child... there is something you should know. Usagi's story may not be mine to tell, but your mother..." Baku's body shimmered into her form and I backed away quickly, releasing his hand in my haste.

"No," I said, shaking my head, I knew the truth. I knew I needed to hate her somewhere deep down. I couldn't cope with the alternative. "No, please, no."

He continued toward me, but after a moment, I stopped backing away and just closed my eyes, falling to my knees in the grass. I looked up at him in my mother's form and it dawned on me just how desperately I'd loved her. Just how much her inability to stand up for me hurt and when she finally did it robbed us of everything. When she'd done the one thing I'd so selfishly wanted... My heart pulsed with pain every time I thought of her outside of the library or without Cole by my side to understand. Baku reached his hand toward my face and I just nodded— defeated, whispers in the wind barely phasing me.

Kneeling before me, he smiled and raised his golden mimic of her hand to cover my eyes. The last thing I saw was golden dust sparkling in the moonlight. As my eyes cleared, I saw something new and it finally occurred to me: 'The Sandman'. Baku reminded me of what I had always thought of as the Sandman, but more. He was ancient and a mix of so many things I hadn't even considered, so many cultures and legends. The thought was fleeting because before I knew it, I saw my mother in front of me, only she appeared to be my age. I recognized her face from the old family photos she'd burned late one night after my father started hurting me.

"She dreamt of you, child. In the nightmares, she saw what was happening coming and didn't know how to stop it, but in the good dreams, the dreams without the nightmares, she took you and your brother and left. She dreamt of leaving him every day he hurt you. She wanted to die each time she heard the sound of impact, but couldn't forget who he'd been before they'd married."

As I watched, she approached a handsome young man with a genuine smile and I took a step closer before I realized... it was my father.

How could he have been anything but what I remembered? His breath had smelled like tobacco or worse each time he'd said my name with a sneer. His knuckles popped each time he angered because his fists clenched so tight they had gone from peach to red to white, the blood stopping short. It was all I was able to see when I thought of him.

If I let myself see the rest...

The forest, everything that happened to my mother; what she'd finally done for us, to protect us. She smiled at the young man and I stared at her. She looked so happy, happier than I had ever seen her. They clasped hands, and somehow without saying anything, they both knew what to do. Looking at each other, a connection passed between them and they ran, smiling and laughing—carefree. How could the monster be this boy? This boy who looked so much like Cole, but with my eyes and lips where Cole had our mother's. What if I became like him? What if I hurt someone? I was not monster, but if he hadn't been...

The idea chilled me to the bone.

The image in front of me changed. "She wanted to run away with you both and buy a bookstore in Manhattan. She'd never been there, but she'd read about it as a child and held on to that memory and a postcard from her sister." Hearing him say the words in her voice held me captive. It didn't hold the same ring, the same mix of self-conscious ness and kindness I always associated with her, but it was her voice and I had missed it.

It's strange, that moment when you realize your parents are people. That they have their own story and their own emotions, and they never were the all-powerful beings you viewed them as when a child. The moment you realize they once fell in love. You don't know them fully and won't get that chance. I didn't want to know the man, but the boy and girl, the happy couple that so free spiritedly ran simply on instinct, just wanting to move and be free, I wanted to know them. I'd always blamed myself or him in turn, switching back and forth as though when I blamed myself it took the sin from him, but now I felt pity for him.

He hadn't just destroyed our family– he'd destroyed himself, too.

"She loved you...more than anything in the world, child, anything except who your father had once been. Watch who you become because your thoughts control your path. Don't let your heart grow cold. That's what he did. He forgot who he was. To justify his actions he continued to break the pieces until he had no resemblance to his true self."

I was in my mother's good dreams now— I could tell because she smiled at Cole and me as we bustled around a small apartment, carefree and laughing, before walking downstairs to a retro little bookstore with meticulous shelving, but all styles and genres from new releases to used classics that fell apart at the spines.

As she took a book from the shelf and looked toward the entrance, a boy entered...my father as he once had been. I started to sob until I couldn't see anything around me, even though I knew I no longer stood in a dream. She loved me... she loved me... she loved me... something about that pulled at me. Something about knowing that she'd felt pain made what my father had done unforgivable. He'd hurt her. She hadn't been the coward I'd thought. She'd been strong, but just... not strong enough. Not until it was too late. Her strength had killed her.

She couldn't give up on him. Ever.

Somehow I'd known, but I just couldn't admit it to myself. I wanted her to love us more, but...the very thing I'd wanted more of from her so desperately was the thing caging her to the last person she'd given it to freely. I didn't want to understand, but I knew it was hard to give love, and even harder to give it freely. Once given freely and used as it had been, it was no wonder she couldn't give it as freely again.

"The forest. She took him camping to see if she could get him back. If not...she was going to leave him," Baku said it so softly I knew it was true.

"No," I sobbed harder, "don't tell me that. No."

I suddenly mourned a woman I hadn't even admitted I'd loved so dearly, whom I'd needed more than anyone in the world. That both Cole and I needed. The idea that she was going to save us, that she wanted to, and that her ultimate dream of happiness included just us being safe and surrounded by books, made me forgive her to some extent.

I knew what she did. We had both guessed.

My heart still harbored the warning of her mistakes, but it also felt a rush of love, affection, and forgiveness. Then, like something inside of me had only just realized it, I knew what my turning off my inner voice meant. I wasn't following in his footsteps, but I wasn't following my own either, and while I still wasn't ready to, knowing that was somehow powerful, like I could be more if I let myself, like his words could one day fade just as the words, 'Beloved husband, father, and friend' would one day wash away from his lying gravestone.

"People change, child. You've seen pain, but remember, just as with this world, it isn't the people you expect. Be on your guard, but don't let your guard consume you."

I nodded into my hands and slowly parted them, surprised at the light that peeked from between them. Already, night had turned back to a blazing sunrise. It was strange the way the world changes when illuminated, but even stranger here. I turned toward the forest, something inside of me telling me to. I saw the stag from the graveyard. He watched me. Looking at him, I felt as I had with the prayer statues. Like I should move toward him as with the tree at the bridge until I felt something wrap around my waist and hold me back.

Arro and Baku saw him, too.

CHAPTER TWELVE

Something unspoken passed between Baku and the stag. The more I observed, the more my confusion grew. Baku looked reverent. His appearance didn't change to mirror the stag's as it had Usagi, Arro, or me, but there was an exchange of sorts, a silent conversation detailing affairs beyond my comprehension.

Suddenly, the exchange ceased and Baku cried out at the stag who raised his head, his eyes regal, unmoving, and unfearing. Baku's tusks came to either side of my body protectively, surrounding me with the most cherished part of any elephant. Weapon's ready to strike anyone who might oppose me. There was something strangely rewarding about having garnered his protection and as I admired his tusks something occurred to me. The stag had antlers like a buck, stag or... a hart.

"The heart of the forest...you meant... Hart? Is..."

"Shhh," Arro admonished.

"I've seen him before."

"What?" Arro turned to me, dismayed.

"I saw him by the graves. He greeted me." I gradually unwrapped Baku's trunk from where it curled around my torso. "And at the hospital before I accidentally..."

"Nooo, child. Pleasssse, you don't understanddd what is happenin'." Baku's voice filled with torment. It stopped me from walking further than halfway across the divide even as the hart felt like my center of gravity, pulling me forward.

"Baku, what is this? What is happening?" Arro's voice apprehensive and as I contemplated, our eyes met.

He wasn't just afraid. He feared for ME. Something beguiled me, like words without a voice. Telling me that it was vital I walk toward the hart to save Cole. This spirit that somehow made peace sweep through me. The kind of peace I'd never felt through the pain and anger. I'd loathed myself. I could see it now and as I did, I could tell the hate wasn't there anymore.

This world had taken it from me one beautiful moment at a time, just as this hart did every time it was near me. It wasn't that it had been caused or taken, simply that this place helped me believe in my core. The real me— the me I wasn't sure I'd actually known before. I stared at Arro and promised myself that I wouldn't forget this moment. The way he watched me... I couldn't remember anyone watching me like that before and I knew it was because of his curse, but something inside of me told me that wasn't all. He saw the barest glimpse of who I was and liked her. It felt freeing– knowing he'd seen that glimpse no one else had and that part of me could be attractive to someone.

I focused on him as I stepped backwards. My eyes didn't waver as they connected with his, even as I shifted toward the hart. I could feel it coming up behind me and stood still, letting him approach. Part of me was terrified of everything happening and another part oddly calm, watching as though I were an onlooker of some strange act; not the girl standing between a kitsune, an elephant, and the spirit of a forest. His breath was warm against my back.

I turned toward him. He stood so close...so wild and untamable.

Again I felt words I could not hear telling me to move and oddly enough my injured arm rose. I felt sharp piercing pain and cried out, but just as soon as it hit, it subsided and my cast was gone.

I will heal Cole if you give me you. You belong here, all you need to do is stay.

Hart mimicked my voice to speak to me, as though he only knew my language through me. I didn't know what to say. It was true; I knew I belonged there in a way I'd never belonged anywhere. This was my home without ever having seen it before. The place I'd been dreaming of when I sat in the graveyard and spoke to my mother or placed flowers at the feet of graves belonging to people I'd never truly known, in the hopes they'd know someone still cared.

"I feel like I know you, but I don't understand how."

You do. You know me. You just never thought you would find me. Usagi is my voice, but she is not a part of me as she once was, she deserves a chance at life, a chance you can one day have too. May I show you? May I change you?

"Change me? What do you mean?"

You belong here. Words... inadequate. Change...

He didn't seem able to communicate what he meant with my voice— my words —but I felt his answer. I felt great change and emotions churning at tornado speeds, then I felt both peace and conflict. With my head nestled between his great antlers I understood.

"Time... I need time to decide," I said the words subconsciously, as though a part of me with more control knew the truth. Even though everything inside of me hungered for the feelings he'd just shown me. But a small part of me reminded myself that if I couldn't love myself now, what difference would it make if I changed?

Cole's gift had been a gift and I needed to think long and hard before turning it away...but I didn't. Not exactly.

Only now.

I knew it was a spur of the moment decision. One I didn't understand, but I also knew I had to do something first. "Will I still be human? Will I get to see Cole again?"

You will get to see your other half but you will not be as you are, you will not be his other piece.

I sent an emotion his way, trying to mimic what he'd done and praying he understood as I turned aside and ran toward Arro. I could feel a rumble rippling through me, almost like a chuckle, if such a thing could shake your soul. I knew he understood. Walking the last few steps to Arro I smiled widely, knowing the gift I had to give and seeing the confusion in his eyes. He hadn't guessed. He didn't even realize that Usagi had revealed the key to his freedom to me, a silly story book twist she'd claimed from my old world that didn't belong in this one.

Before he came to his senses, I quickly stretched on my tip toes and used my good arm to grasp his neck, pulling him the last few inches. I let my lips caress his and his arms circled my waist, pulling me closer. It took him a fraction of a second to register what was happening, but once he had he kissed back. At first tenderly, sweetly even, and then with more passion. I'd only planned on kissing him to return to him what was rightfully his, but somehow it had turned into something more the second our lips touched. I'd never been kissed before. I'd never realized just how wonderful it would feel as it sent warm static unreservedly through my entire body.

I ached for more and as much as I knew I should pull back, I didn't. I didn't want this to end and somehow, it was him. It wasn't just the feelings sweeping through me. It was Arro and the way he looked at me. I didn't trust him or think anything would come of it, but I could have this one moment, he owed me at least that much for giving him back the thing he wanted most. His hand brushed against the side of my face so softly my knees shook in a way they never had before; with excitement. I had to fight not to waiver and instead deepened the kiss further.

After a few more moments, I knew I had to pull away. I was breathless, my heart fluttering so fast I couldn't help but wonder if he could hear it beating like hummingbird wings. I smiled when I realized he was breathless too. Instead of seeing the gratitude I'd expected in his eyes, I saw hunger. It thrilled me. Sending a shiver down my spine and spreading warmth through my chest. We watched each other and when I smiled, he realized what I'd done.

He took my hand in his and stared deep into my eyes. "Thank you."

The words were short and his voice overcome with emotion. Somehow it seemed fitting. I didn't want to hear more than that. I just wanted to know he was free. I could give him at least that much in exchange for helping me find a way to bring Cole back. My fingers touched my lips. I could still feel his touch lingering on my skin, his warmth still a part of me.

Then before my eyes he started to change. First just colors, his hair got an orange tint to it and half of it went darker while the front of it lightened to a red orange in a luminous ombre. His skin paled and his lips darkened. He still looked human so far, but not the way he had a moment before. He shook out like a dog might shake off water and in almost an instant, empty clothes lay on the ground and a divine fox stood in front of me.

Kissing Arro felt amazing and right, but something about the idea of kissing this creature was intimidating. As though I thought of them as two separate entities even though I knew they were one. He looked so majestic and strange, dark fur climbing up his paws, yet white fur stirred along his chest and much of his face. The coloring of his human form made sense to me, his pale skin and orange and black hair. His eyes were still the same this way, still soulful and human, almost too human for his majestic form. As though he'd been stuck for far too long and couldn't completely shake it.

He came to me and I stumbled back a step. He stood taller than me, and unlike many foxes had four tails, rising above him in a thick autumn fan. He froze before I could take another step back and I stilled, watching him. My instincts kicked in when he looked like this. I couldn't help my trepidation. He was of the forest and I wasn't. My old fears returned and I looked down, overwhelmed. I had to fight to stay still, but put up a front and raised my face to smile. When I did he stood before me as a human again, still pulling his shirt over his head.

"Baku, what's going on?" he asked.

Baku closed his eyes, his head moving from side to side as though what he truly wished to shake free lay inside his mind.

"He wants to make her the spirit. All because of that selfish petulant woman."

When he spoke he reflected Usagi and everything came crashing down on me. He was right. That was what the hart wanted. The change I'd felt. He wanted me to be a part of him and this forest– his voice. He wanted me to stay so Usagi could be freed.

"It's the only way to save Cole…" Something in my eyes caused defeat to reflect in Baku's, even in Usagi's form.

"You are wrong, but it doesn't matter, you are marked. Your hand, when he blessed you, now when you die you will come to this realm, rather than move on."

I looked down at my now working arm, darkened with shadows like Usagi's only were dotted with small stars, roaming across my skin.

"This place feels like a part of me." I breathed the words out softly and knew I didn't fully comprehend. I knew this was all too much for anyone to understand, but the idea of Cole getting to live the life that he always wanted drove me back, step by step.

"You don't understand what you're giving up, child. One day you will feel as Usagi does. One day you will want to be free and Cole will be gone. You'll have to watch him age and die. Just as I care for child after child and see them pass. It's torture, Lily. It hurts more than anything you can imagine."

"But it helps them. What you do. It helped me. I just need... I want good. I want happy and I don't care who gets it as long as someone does. Who am I kidding? If Cole dies I won't be happy here or anywhere else. I can feel it: the hole inside of me."

"What will fill it when you give his heart back to him? Ask yourself, ask him." He motioned to the hart who didn't react. As though our conversation was nothing but a formality. He knew, as I did, that I'd chosen.

"This place...Me... the me I forced to leave so long ago. I just... I need this." I spoke and Baku bowed his head.

"It's yours to choose, child. I don't want you to leave. You're kind and lost and you do feel 'right' here, but child... I watched Usagi. I saw her journey and it was one of misery. Whether by my touch or his, see her story first. You must enter this future with open eyes. I wouldn't wish to reveal her torment to anyone, but it's not a thing easily understood any other way."

I knew it should matter to me–that Baku's words should've penetrated my resolve, but I came here to save Cole. Even then, as I was close enough to feel the hart's warm breath on my back. I could only feel bitter relief at the idea of seeing Cole's eyes. I wanted to watch him laugh and hear his voice. I ached to be the hero and not the victim.

I felt the memories that held pieces of me together for so long, the days he and I lay together in the graveyard and had our picnics. Making up stories about the graves surrounding us. I remembered his soft touch on my shoulder each time he could see my mind wandering and just wanted to bring me back. He'd made my life beautiful. He knew no one else would, so he took it upon himself.

He saved me.

Now, I could save him.

CHAPTER THIRTEEN

I will do it. I can save him... I can save him... I can save him." I kept repeating it under my breath, a reminder to keep the fear at bay. I didn't want to let my doubts in, to remember that I feared forests and was asking to become a part of one. To remember the horrible thing my mother had done. To realize I may get to see Cole again, but I'd have no idea what I was, what I'd become, or if he would be able to understand.

I tried to imagine myself as Usagi; wearing some bewitching piece of clothing with bold natural ink painted across my face, but I just couldn't see it. It didn't fit me. I could feel the hart move it's forehead to mine and my head nuzzled between his great antlers again.

This is her story. Usagi's. Once you have seen it you can decide yourself. I would not want to anger the dream keeper and he is right; this is not a decision to be made by me.

It belongs to you.

His voice reflected my own again and for a moment I felt like I was falling, but too terrified to dare move. "Hello?" I called into the darkness. It surrounded me and although I couldn't escape and most might panic; this was my time. Darkness had always belonged to me. That was it, wasn't it? There was something about that. Something important. I didn't know why, but I could feel it.

Something about shadows.

I saw something moving in the darkness. He reflected my voice.

"Only a human can be my voice in this world. Usagi was a human once. Before she'd been named Usagi, she was just a girl named Sachiko whose family had forgotten her in a fire caused by a fox."

"By a fox. By Arro?"

"They've hated each other longer than they can remember, but it never started with Arro. He distrusted humans, but he never meant to hurt her. He never meant to hurt anyone. Her grudge against the part he played in her death for so long is all that caused his own grudge against her. He watched her curiously and that curiosity was his own downfall."

"What do you mean?"

"Watch…"

Warmth rolled over my body and I could only see red, orange, and yellow blurring into one. The heat got overwhelming, no longer just skin deep. Then I saw a girl. People were running and she hid in the corner, afraid to cross the flames. A couple and their son ran, she cried when she heard their screams outside. The house looked small and wooden. I couldn't tell what era this was, but I knew it was a time before what I'd studied, likely in Asia based off of Usagi's taste in clothes since and her name. I wasn't sure where.

I wanted to go to her, wrap my arms around her and run, but I already knew there was nothing I could do. Sachiko, Usagi before she became a spirit. I still went to her; I couldn't help myself or fight the instinct. Seeing her fear I didn't want to. I just wanted to comfort her and heal her pain. Some part of me, even knowing this was the past, desperate to help. Then I realized her family screamed from outside… they'd died out there; even if she ran, it would make no difference.

"How did this happen?" I whispered in horror.

In a jarring instant the scene changed and I saw a fox running through the woods, his exquisite amber coat shining brightly. So young, too small and courageous to be a true adult fox. *Arro?* I watched as he entered a clearing, curiously following a young Sachiko. He watched her and so far she hadn't noticed. Somehow the scene felt unusual. The fox curious about the child and ignorant of the fact that she held danger to him as all humans do. Just as the lone barefooted child wandered through a forest too curious to bother seeing the fox that spelled danger to her as well— watching her —wanting to understand her.

Something about the idea that they were both natural enemies who didn't realize it yet caught my attention; it wasn't just that they didn't know, while natural instinct might tell them otherwise, these two didn't have to be a danger to each other. Yet, somehow they were. Then I heard it, a third set of footsteps coming up from beside them. I saw him, but neither of them did; a hunter. The man had a bow and arrow and realization swept over me... Arro. His spirit name was a cruel joke at his expense. Willow had mentioned it, but it hadn't sunk in. Every time someone said his name it held a constant reminder of what transpired here.

I didn't even have time to move, time to have any instincts kick in or get past the shock in the time it took the hunter to draw his arrow, take aim, and shoot. I gasped as I heard it hit its mark. It skewered his tail, pinning him to the ground. He started to writhe, trying to break free. I turned away only to see Sachiko running through the woods.

The scene stopped and for a moment I had my precious darkness back as though the hart knew that I needed it. I couldn't stand to see anything hurt, let alone an animal. My heart started to beat normally again, slowing until I could breathe evenly. Somehow knowing it was Arro made it closer to me, somehow more vivid, as though I were watching something I shouldn't have.

When the scene reappeared, the hunter snared Arro and carried him as he ran after Sachiko, calling out to her in a language I couldn't understand. Somehow I didn't feel like I needed to. The meaning was obvious, he must have been her father, and the man I'd seen leave the house without her. When they got back to the house she ran in, and through to another corner as the man set up a makeshift cage next to the hearth. He then followed after her, but I could only watch Arro, so young, frightened and innocent. He'd done nothing, but he'd pay the price for his curiosity just as the hart said.

He started to check his surroundings, trying to find a way to get out. He rammed against the sides, trying to break free and the voices from the other room covered the clattering and breaking of the branches that bound him. When they fell away, I covered my mouth in horror realizing how the fire started. The cage was wood and it scattered in pieces across the floor, hearth, and wall.

The fox ran, trying to find a way out of the house and finally found an opening, leaving the fire in his wake. Knowing what happened to Usagi just after, I decided to follow him outside instead and when I walked through the door could see the fire had started to consume one wall and spread to the next house. Then the screaming started. Rushing back into the house, I saw Sachiko's family gather in the living room and remain oblivious to her only feet away from them.

She watched the fire and this time I saw what she looked at, the few pieces of the cage that hadn't been wood. The arrow on the other side of the room still untouched, mocking her as she looked at it. I could see why she hated Arro. And while I knew it was wrong... I could understand it.

Her family left her. Possibly thinking she ran behind them, but somehow I knew that wouldn't occur to her. She wouldn't care because she didn't get to leave with them. Then I saw what she did next, instead of running to the door she raced the opposite direction and found a window in another room to crawl through. Finding her way out, she ran without looking back as tears streamed down her face.

She didn't dare stop. She just kept running. I was struck by how strong that was of her. The fire spread to the trees and somehow she'd known it would. Somehow she knew to just keep running as fast as her young body would carry her, even when she tripped over a large root rising up out of the ground and cut her leg she continued. Her face... Her strength... It shouldn't have been dazzling to me, but something about it was and I could understand why she'd become a spirit with that kind of inner beauty.

Then I saw Arro running beside her, hidden in the trees. Death chasing them down as the forest burned around them. Hadn't he left? Hadn't he run far from the source of his pain? I don't know how long they ran like that. The fire gaining on them one blazing tree at a time. They never even realized. All this time and they still hated each other when they'd been the same.

They were abandoned, then trapped and just wanted freedom. Each one the downfall of the other...

They'd been running so long and I'd been so enraptured that I didn't realize she couldn't last much longer, she was only a young child. The forest started to change, the fire disappearing until it wasn't the same forest. How did people enter the spirit world? Where had the fire gone? They couldn't possibly have out run it. There were different gateways to the forest, but did they all lead to the same place and where might these openings be? Was it possible they'd just run through one? Because the trees were ever so softly turning violet as they went, the coloring deepening with each tree they passed.

They came here together.

Then I saw the stag, the hart of the forest, standing there like a guardian before a few scattered statues. Not as crowded as the ones I'd seen after crossing the bridge. He walked with Usagi and then time passed strangely, like I watched everything on fast forward, making me dizzy. When the girl fell asleep curled against his side, the fox revealed himself and when the stag and fox touched noses the fox changed into what I now knew as Arro, the large four tailed kitsune in all its glory.

He walked away, entering the spirit world in a way Sachiko had been too hesitant to.

"She was lost, broken, but she, like you, had passion. She had so much life left unlived; life that could fuel this forest. I couldn't leave her that way."

"It's strange. That girl is Usagi, but it isn't."

"There's more." The hart warned and the darkness welcomed me again. Then, I saw her smiling up at the stag the way one might expect a young child to watch their parent. The stag seemed happy, paternal in return. He truly had raised her. "She wasn't aging and she noticed. She answered a prayer using the stones and when she saw the woman, she wanted so desperately to be beautiful. To be that woman and have her life and the love she got to witness day after day– but nothing ever changed."

Seeing the girl bring her hand away from the stone and dip her head, trying to hide the sorrow welling underneath the surface. I could see it, I could feel how badly she wanted it and before my eyes, it happened.

She grew and grew without pain until she looked like the painted woman I'd come to see in this world. She was so happy, looking down at herself tears spilled from her eyes as she spun and spun and I heard her say her new name, "Usagi", adopted from the woman who had prayed to her ancestors. She squealed in delight as she threw herself at the hart and wrapped her arms around him lovingly.

"She was happy for so long, even when she saw Arro and blamed him. She wanted to be here more than anything. Until one day she answered Kaede's prayer. He said things...things she understood all too well and for the first time she wondered what it would be like to be loved by a man. Then she realized she wasn't sure who she was without this place and part of her wanted to find out."

I watched the woman I'd seen, the brilliant goddess-like human being who swayed with the wind, a part of this place...peaceful as she walked through the trees toward the prayer statues. She let her hand brush against one and heard Kaede's voice. "Please, whoever it's out there listening. I don't need some spectacular life, I just... I save people every day... all day and as much as I love what I do, I see how happy they are when they find out their loved one is okay and I don't have that. I never have. I've never felt that kind of passion, the kind that would make a grown sane man walk through the flames for the woman he loves. I saw it today and I want it. I want it more than anything, but... I still need to help. I feel so damn selfish right now, but...whoever is out there. I want that kind of love, the crazy stupid kind. Even if I stand here and spend every day for the next forty years saving people, let me feel it at least once...just once."

I watched her face and was a fool for having questioned why she would ever want Kaede. He was a passionate man, a man who, like

Cole, had only ever wanted to help. Even hell and gone from society he found a way to continue to help everyone around him. The passion in his voice— the pleading. It felt like it cut through my heart, but I knew that kind of love, a love strong enough that a person might venture through another world on what could be a suicide mission just to save the one good thing in their life. But now... I can't say he is the only good thing... Not knowing what Baku had told me about my mother.

Not knowing she did it for us.

Imagining the future we were headed to. It was meant to be everything we never got to have. I did have more to my life than just him... it just didn't take away from what he meant to me or the debt I owed my own heart, knowing everything he had been. Like Kaede, he only ever wanted to help, but unlike Kaede, he always held a burning love in his heart for everyone he met and every life he touched no matter how many times he'd been turned away.

Relentless, he never grew bitter.

Usagi never realized what she missed until that moment. I could tell as I watched her expression change, the ink always swelling around her hands lifting and filling her body as her emotions spread through her. This time instead of stripes of blue or red she swirled a torrent of color as the emotions exploded and paint splattered every inch of her. A kaleidoscope of color creating small galaxies with Usagi as the canvas. He was her reflection, he wanted exactly what she wanted, but would never put into words.

As I watched her skin, I wanted to call her the painted woman. Her emotions on the surface, a need and eagerness for the kind of life she'd never had a chance to live. She might only get a chance to if I became a spirit here. If I was willing to trade my bright beautiful future for her and wait for the next poor soul to wander here and take my place before I could truly live out there again, if I wanted to.

"Will she be released if I become your shadow? Your voice? Can she truly leave this place and live a happy and full life with Kaede and Willow?"

"She can leave this place and live with them, her happiness and fulfillment depend on what she does with that opportunity," the voice said as though it had some doubt.

I didn't. Seeing her there, the way she wanted the outside world– I'd felt that before. I'd sat in my library staring at books filled with pictures from around the world just wishing beyond anything I could be there and get to see it with my own eyes. Wishing with everything that I had. It was all I wanted, all I needed was a chance and I'd have taken it without a second thought.

I'd have run.

That realization hit me hard. I'd have left Cole behind if it meant getting to believe the way he always wanted me to. I had faith that he could live without me. That he could thrive. Now, I needed that hope because I hadn't thought about what this might do to him. Would he come back whole? What happens when you are in a coma without hope of waking? What happens when the machines take over and you leave? How would he live without me? He was so strong, but...

Here I stood wishing this pain on him and forgetting the look on his face when he begged for me to be saved. Forgetting he only saved me because losing me felt like it killed him too. We were in the same boat and suddenly as my thoughts turned rational, I realized that boat was sinking. I only had one way to save him, I thought I had a choice, but I didn't. We were two halves of the same coin that fate had expected to flip and instead were here spinning it round and round like a dreidel and never allowing it to stop long enough to land.

My mind wandered as I watched Usagi, her beauty no longer fazing me as it once did. Underneath it all she was just a girl like me who never got to grow up, and yet... had grown up too quickly. Who'd seen that sometimes people were left behind or hurt by those they loved most. "You are so beautiful," I whispered to the memory, but it wasn't her physical attributes or even the galaxies written across her skin, it was her eagerness to live. The one thing I'd let go of in all of this.

The one thing I'd forgotten had always been a part of me. "I want to free her. I want to save Cole... I want... I just want so much."

Do you know why humans are the only ones able to be my voice and only once they come to me and agree? Some others here were human once, but they aren't now. It has to be some-one who makes this choice. The choice you are in the process of making.

"Why?"

Because of that hunger for life, it sustains this forest. Without one human spirit this forest dies and all of us eventually go along with it.

I halted in shock. How could anyone be so important? Was he saying I'd be sustaining the forest if I were to stay here? ... He wanted me here? I was...wanted.

"There is more you should see," he said, his voice still my own, but this time he used tones I did not know how. A tone filled with emotion, but void of it on the surface.

Usagi stood at the edge of the forest watching through the trees. I had to take a step closer to see what she saw because of the dense foliage. Willow.

I watched as blue ink tears trailed down Usagi's cheeks and buried themselves beneath her kimono. She wanted to run to Willow. I could see it in everything about her posture. She was having to use all of her strength not to sprint from this forest to her daughter, who paced the length of the bridge, fiddling with a necklace that looked like some sort of piece of stone or metal tied by a leather cord. Usagi collapsed and turned away, unable to watch any longer.

I wished I could put my arms around her as she started to sob with so much sorrow it felt closer to what I'd have expected from the child in the fire. But fire didn't burn the way a broken heart did, it didn't sear as deeply as watching someone you love think so little of you.

She didn't leave because she isn't willing to sacrifice the forest and all of the souls she has come to love, for her own happiness.

I saw the stag approach her and curl itself around her as it had the young girl who restlessly hadn't been able to sleep so many centuries earlier. She wrapped her arms around him and cried. The hart allowed me for just a moment to feel their communication, her desperate fervor and her heart pleading with him to be freed. Begging the way one might for their life if they did not believe anything lay after.

It wasn't without love or she would have left, instead it was filled with it. Overwhelming her. She loved this place the way I did, in a way that filled her with wonder and made her want to be a better person. But she loved Willow and Kaede so desperately and the true difference lay in that the forest was here, living and breathing and eternal, but her daughter and her love...she could feel them dying.

My heart broke with hers. I shattered realizing I might one day feel that way. I'd watch Cole die and hear his prayers when he hurt. I had no guarantee his life would be the wonderful existence I'd dreamt up for him. But then again... I thought of Arro, Baku and even the spirit currently surrounding me, who in this memory was so loving, giving, and compassionate.

I belonged here, I'd been the one born to die, not him.

Never him.

"We are running out of time. He is fading." I heard my own voice, but only half my voice, the rest communicated through the emotions. The feeling of impending deadline.

"Hurry, do it," I told him, "please."

"Are you sure, child?" I heard Baku's voice and was back in the field.

"Yes, hurry! You can't let him go and let Usagi be trapped here. I can't... Please," I begged, watching the hart stand inhumanly still, then its head lifted and I could feel how bittersweet this was for him; like losing a child and gaining another in the same moment.

He wanted her to live a happy and full life, but he wanted me here, my passion and eagerness. It hurt him letting her go. She was his, a part of him like Cole and I were a part of each other. On a level we couldn't explain and never even bothered to try.

The hart looked at Arro and something passed between them. Arro nodded and he in turn looked to Baku as the same transpired. "I will tell them we will meet them at the threshold," Baku said, taking my form for a moment before he changed into something I wasn't sure how to describe, incredibly fast as he darted into the forest, much like the dragon from before.

The stag turned to me. I glanced at Arro who stared, his eyes a mix of emotions I couldn't understand. I was always better at reading emotions through voices and words than expressions.

"I'm ready." I could feel my breath quicken with anticipation.

The forest has no rules for its heart.

The one thing that truly cannot be controlled.

Yet, there are a few simple truths.

1. There is only one heart, though there are many who live in the shadows of the forest.

2. The truth is never simple or easy. There is no black and white, just gray.

3. Acceptance is a choice and an emotion.

It's a state of being.

An undeniable rush of understanding.

CHAPTER FOURTEEN

As the hart's head rose the world around me rippled. It faded, but just as quickly as it did there was an explosion inside of me. My insides burned with passion that spread through me, rising to the surface and overwhelming everything I remembered about my past. The memories remained, but my hunger for this life, for this place felt palpable, physical. Even my emotions for Arro were becoming clearer; I wanted to be loved and he was the first person to look at me as though he could, as though I were something desirable.

This place needed me and all I'd ever wanted was to be needed.

Cole never truly needed me. I couldn't help but feel joy as I connected to the stag. So unusual, like the connection I had to Cole transferred to another, but amplified. I could feel his emotions a step behind my own like a subconscious part of me. I wasn't sure what else might be different until I felt the hart's shock. My connection to him wasn't like his connection to Usagi; it ran deeper and more encompassing, more natural. It felt as right to him as it did to me.

I could feel his emotions swelling. The sorrow of letting Usagi go outweighed by the thrill our connection gave him and his knowledge that she would be given the fate she had bartered for.

"You have thought of yourself as a monster for so long," he told me, seeing through my barriers, "but you are not. Look what you have created."

He backed away and I opened my eyes to see him rear up on his hind legs as his antlers extend further, his size larger than it was before. Seeing the strength I'd given him, I found something in myself I wasn't sure I had before— faith. Faith in who I was at my core. Faith that I wasn't the same kind of person my father had been just because he had filled me with anger; because it could be a choice— to release myself from the anger, my cages, unlike Usagi toward Arro. To let it all go.

I looked around and the forest had grown. The trees stretching toward the sky, the light brighter and the color more vivid. I could feel the hart sending emotions to me. Telling me in his own way that I needed to get to Cole now and give back what had been taken or my choice would mean so much less than it had the possibility to. I bowed my head and let my gratitude fill my heart as I took Arro's hand and ran. He led me, but some part of me knew this forest and the direction without even meaning to. That's when I noticed the hand that held his looked black with ink like Usagi's. I cared but I didn't, the only thing on my mind was the countdown I could feel the hart focusing on. Reminding me as he led me.

I could feel Cole cross the bridge and held the trees back, not allowing them to send him any pain in fear it might kill him. The hart finally accepted Kaede just enough for him to stay to help. Willow walked in as naturally as Usagi would have, somehow part of this forest in a way the hart never intended. I ran faster than I'd even known I could as the countdown ticked down too quickly. I wasn't going to make it.

"Arro…" I pled, my voice strained and in an instant he tossed me into the air with ease and become a fox below me. I had barely enough time to lean forward and circle my arms around him before he sprang into an all out run. We could make it… thanks to Arro, we would make it.

"Thank you," I whispered against the wind, not sure if he could hear. I'd have to give up the last part of Cole left inside of me if I wanted to free us both. What once made me feel like we were two halves had been encompassed by the hart of the forest. I was his shadow and he mine. The steady rhythm in my chest the only part of Cole I had left. I could feel the risk the forest took giving me this power and it honored me to have the forest's trust. We were passing the statues so fast they blurred in my vision. I could feel each one the largest emanating the most power, the whispers of prayers calling out to me. The violet trees reaching toward me as we went.

I'd make it. We would make it. We had to. When I saw him, he lay on a makeshift emergency gurney and Kaede gawked at the trees star struck. Willow noticed us first and started to back away. "Change back," I told Arro. "She doesn't know it's you."

He changed quickly and ducked behind a tree. I remembered he had clothes stashed somewhere to change into whenever he went back and forth before, like when he brought me across the bridge to begin with. I ran to Cole, and Willow kept asking questions I ignored. I could answer them later. I reached for him and just before touching him saw Usagi running toward us. I knew I didn't have time to figure things out, so let myself hold my brother and release the part of him that belonged to me for the last few days. The part of himself he was willing to live or die without to save me.

For a moment, holding him in my arms we were one again. Our heart, one heart. Our battles shared from a time before forests, talking foxes, and spirits. *What if this heart had been changed too greatly during my travels for him to accept it back?* That this would all be for nothing. Then I remembered how far we'd come, how much I'd grown, and how much I now knew and believed possible. Feeling my faith, I reached out, I was willing to break my heart in two for him as he'd done for me. I could feel the heart leave me and for just a moment couldn't fight the shock, the loss of him inside of my chest. For the briefest of seconds I heard chimes again and pain flowed through me, louder now, but as I watched his eyes open, it was replaced by a kind of joy I hadn't felt before, so brilliant inside of me that I thought I might burst with light.

I didn't look up even as I heard Willow say, "I don't understand."

I guessed she looked on at the entire situation, but I couldn't see anything but Cole. When he raised his hand groggily to rub at his eyes like he always had when he first woke up, I cried out in happiness and in doing so a sprinkle of clear warm rain water started to drizzle down on us. I smiled knowing this world cried with me. I'd never have to feel alone again, even with the loss of the one person who meant so much to me. Now... I meant something to me too. I could be myself without him and something about that felt empowering.

I hadn't lost him yet.

"I am so happy you're okay." My arms still held him to me.

"He will still need time to heal," Kaede warned, but I didn't care because at least he would heal.

He lay in front of me with open blinking eyes and that silly look of bewilderment. It wasn't the forest yet, the realization hadn't settled in. It was just his morning wonderment at waking. When he asked, "What happened?" I felt whole knowing he would be okay.

He saw me and our eyes met. First he only focused on my eyes and I knew they were the same as always. Then I saw my arms, I was covered in galaxies of color as Usagi once was. I tried to reel it in, but couldn't contain my joy. Somehow he didn't freak, even though to be honest if our places were reversed I would've. I'd never had much of a poker face.

"I could feel it. My heart remembers something... I don't know how to explain it... A journey... your journey," he said his voice still rough, then I noticed Willow shrieking.

"No, you deserted us!" she cried at her mother and I turned to look.

Usagi stood before her daughter as a woman now, no ink tracing her hands or wrists as it once had and her tears no longer blue ink, but plain water. Even her grace and grandeur had paled, somehow I liked her better this way. The mask stripped to reveal the true beauty within, the human being underneath it all.

"The forest was dying without her," I explained, "Along with all the spirits in it."

Arro looked at me in shock. Apparently he hadn't known. When I looked from Kaede to Willow and back again, I could see that Kaede himself wasn't sure. He couldn't stop watching Usagi.

"Your shadows, they're gone," he said, walking forward.

Cole sat up now, so I tried not to worry about Kaede leaving his side. Seeing my worry, Arro stood by Cole and started talking to him quietly.

"Yes," Usagi answered and seeing her face the emotions were evident even without the color that had once run beneath her skin.

"That means..." Kaede's statement cut off and ended up being more of a question. He knew the answer, but he wouldn't voice his fragile hope.

"We can be together. I can leave now. My spirit has been released in exchange for another."

She looked at me and I could tell she was grateful. I thought back to her begging the stag and knew that just as much as she had begged, she felt equally as grateful to us both. She was not the kind of person to feel in half measures. The hart knew it. Kaede turned to me, seeing the shadows underneath my skin that spiraled restlessly. I was mostly my normal self, but like Usagi my shadows mainly graced my hands and I'd venture a guess my legs as well.

Looking down to inspect them further for the first time, I noticed the arm from the cast appeared different from the other, the shadows swirled with more force and instead of the black of Usagi they were like small blue and violet galaxies reminding me of the night sky that had welcomed the stars of the spirits when the graves broke. The violet so similar to the trees of this walkway that I couldn't help but smile remembering the way the forest had welcomed me. The way I knew them somehow in some subtle way and they knew me.

"You..."

"I needed to save Cole. This... saved each of us. This way Cole lived and Usagi would be freed."

"I am no longer Usagi."

"Sachiko," I said smiling.

"It has been so long since I heard anyone say my name... It is fitting that you be the first."

I looked over to Willow, her own skin writhed with color. "Willow, your mom loves you more than anything. Now, she can be with you. She did this for you both."

I looked from Kaede to Willow, knowing this wouldn't be easy for them to accept. I was surprised to see Kaede's confusion soften to resolve as he went to her, sweeping her into a tight embrace and spinning her around him, accepting her without question, as though the fact that they belonged to each other held the only answers he needed. Their love had always been genuine.

Willow watched and while at first her confusion grew, something softened in her as well when she saw how happy her father looked. When their spinning stopped, Sachiko looked to Willow insecurely, wondering what she might think, say, or do.

"I love you," Sachiko said softly and Willow's face melted, her lips dipping at the sides as though she were trying not to cry.

"I... I don't know..." she stuttered.

The casual confidence of the girl from the hospital gone, her emotions too close to the surface to hide. I could understand it now. She was a part of the forest and always had been, she couldn't help but have her emotions close to the surface. She was the girl with her emotions literally written across her skin, ever moving and ever changing, but always visible.

We could see it, the confusion, the passion, the anger, the sadness, all too visible on this side of the bridge. Then I realized how much of a relief it might be for her to be away from here. Getting to have the life she looked at in magazines and be out in the world. Getting to have friends and never worry about someone seeing her emotions unless she chose to reveal them. But would she miss them? The spirits? Would she ever want to come back and if she wanted... could she?

I could feel the hart's response. She would always have a place here. She would carry a piece of the forest with her forever. "Willow, you can go now, you, Kaede, and your mother can leave this place and see the world. You can go to school and have friends. Go shopping and go to the movies. You can see that world and know that you always carry a piece of this one with you. You can always come back."

"Always?"

"Always," I said, smiling as she smirked, her confidence back again and her shadows under control as she walked to her mother and hesitantly held out her hand. Sachiko wrapped her arms around her fiercely instead and Willow hesitated only a moment or two before returning the embrace.

"I always wanted you here," Willow said so softly into Sachiko's hair that I almost didn't hear.

"I always wanted to stay. To be by your side, but I'd have been killing... I know you don't understand now, but I can tell you everything. We have time now. We have the rest of our lives together if you both want me." Her words were heartfelt and raw and now Kaede, Sachiko, and Willow were holding each other, all a mix of emotions that brought tears to my eyes. I turned back to Cole who watched me, his own emotions unreadable to me for the first time in our lives.

"I feel different," he said when I went to him and I stopped myself from choking, to force the shadowy ink under my skin not to show my own feelings which were always so evident to him. "I'd have paid the price, you know, Lil?"

"I know," I said and realized I forgave him for making the pact that lead me here and I hoped he could forgive me for breaking it. Here where I'd grown and learned so much, even if there was still so much left to learn. Here where I slowly learned to set the pain aside and understand that some things wouldn't go according to plan and that sometimes when plans fall apart you end up with an even more beautiful result than the ones you intended.

"What will happen now?" he asked me.

I noticed he kept switching between watching my face and my hands. I had no idea. "I don't know."

"You have to stay here now though? Like what you said about that woman?" It was strange to hear him refer to her as 'that woman' when just a few hours ago she was the kind of person whose very presence would have commanded respect.

"Yes."

"Can I stay too?"

"For a while, but eventually... No. I had to change to save you, but it means I can't go back."

"Can I change too?" Cole asked earnestly.

He didn't want to leave my side and while I thought about my own emotions and vaguely of his, I hadn't thought that time might not have passed the same way for him. He saw me dying and made a desperate pact and now he had a life he hadn't expected to have in the blink of an eye. I hadn't thought he might want to stay here with me. I hadn't even considered that we could both stay.

He isn't ready yet. He still has more to do.

"Cole, you don't really want that, do you?" I could feel that the forest might accept him, but only because of his pact. It wasn't the way it was for me. I needed the forest just as much as it needed me, as though it were a part of me crying out to be heard and once I connected with it I was more myself with than without it. Even more so than when I'd thought of Cole as my other half. I didn't need someone else to be whole now and I didn't know how to explain that to him, that even if he stayed he wouldn't belong here. He was meant to be alive. To help out there.

"I did this so that you could go back. So that you could have that life you have always wanted and leave behind the shadows of the past that hung over our heads. But... I also did this for me, I guess. Once I'd seen this place, I didn't want to leave."

He hadn't even listened to me; he'd been staring at Baku. I couldn't help myself, I laughed. It was absurd and I knew it probably wasn't the best choice, but it was just so fulfilling to see Cole's face in that moment, the shock and awe. He had only seen all of us as humans and myself as the oddest among us now. Baku nodded his head at Cole when I turned toward him.

Before speaking he mirrored me and I gasped. I hadn't realized how much this place had changed me since the last time he'd shown me.

I liked it. I liked what I saw and I wasn't not sure I'd ever thought that before about myself as a whole. Not in the self-righteous way, just, in that I didn't mind being me. I liked who I was and respected the decisions I'd made and that's all anyone could ask of their self. I knew that now. For so many years I'd thought, *If I were just someone else* and now looking at myself I could see I'd been wrong. Everyone had something beautiful inside of them.

"How long can I stay?"

I asked the hart how long Cole and I had together and his response once again held inaudible emotions that spread through me like warmth, but not without admonition.

One ceremony.

CHAPTER FIFTEEN

I swallowed hard realizing how much I'd miss him. I'd lose him again and only get to hear his prayers or see Baku play pretend again, purely for my own comfort. I wasn't going to waste a single moment. And…I wouldn't let him know. I'd bear the burden of the timer ticking down inside my chest.

"We have to leave," Sachiko said and for a moment I wanted to curse her, to vehemently deny it even though I knew it to be true. I should've known she would know.

"We have time. I want Cole to see this world before he leaves," I said and when she looked into my eyes I saw that some part of what she had been remained.

Her eyes bore into mine and she knew. I could tell she thought I'd be endangering them by letting them stay too long, but I wouldn't risk it and I wouldn't risk Cole feeling any pain for the sake of my own greed.

"I promise I'll let you know when it's time to go, but for now, we do have time." I tried to sound majestic rather than cryptic so that Cole might blame it on my newfound change, but the truth of the matter was that I hadn't changed all that much. I still carried the shadows of my old life like galaxies across my skin, my mind still wandered and while I felt more content, I still had a hunger for the life this place filled itself with. The life Cole was filled with too. His eagerness and kindness. I wanted it all and maybe for just a few hours I could actually have it all.

This place would have to be enough for me after that. I could feel the shadows dancing like ink across my skin. It wasn't quite like Willow or Usagi's, it made designs on occasion, but as quickly as they appeared they left. A cherry blossom here and gone again, then a seahorse or something else that somehow attached to a memory. I wouldn't waste my precious time with Cole thinking about it. Warmth crawled up my back and I could already guess it was a design, Arro was the only one close enough to see. He came up behind me and wrapped his arms around me, covering my back completely.

"Don't think about pain, it shows bruises," he whispered ever so softly, the warmth of his breath sweeping across my cheek. I may have become the voice of the forest, but I was no goddess like Usagi. I didn't walk with new grace and I was anything but immune to his touch. I could still feel our kiss lingering on my lips. I let myself lean back into him, so enriched by the comfortable way we were touching that the shadows receded.

"Thank you," I whispered and I knew that he could see the effect he had on me. The way he managed to calm my soul.

"How long do we have?" Sachiko asked.

CHAPTER SIXTEEN

s I stood, I decided to tell her.

"One ceremony," I whispered.

Cole managed to stand, but stumbled into my back. As he was about to pull away, I wrapped my arms around him tighter and pressed our chests against one another's, heart to heart. We were the same height, the same size, our features were so similar. He had a future and now I did too. One with Arro, beauty and adventure, but also the realization that it wouldn't include him was slowly sinking in because somehow never having been without him, it was too difficult to comprehend.

He could feel it. I could tell. I knew the moment he realized why I held him that way and his grip on me tightened. Heroes weren't always like the spirits who end up here as Kaede had told me, sometimes they were the person who picked you up when you fell, whose touch never hurt and whose intentions were always pure even if they made mistakes. Sometimes a hero was someone who just kept trying even when it seemed like the world was a horrible place and nothing could fix it.

"Cole, you're my hero."

"Lily," he chuckled lightly, but I could hear his broken heart through it, like a chink in his armor, "You're my hero. You always have been. Being here, you see it– your strength, but I saw it there. I saw it before. Always."

"Pfft." I rolled my eyes, but when we pulled away I smiled at him, hoping he knew how much his words meant to me. How much being seen could mean when you knew what it was like to be invisible.

"Then I suppose we should show them the ceremony?" Sachiko asked.

She smiled when I nodded, but I could see she was conflicted. She knew I needed a moment, but she also knew there wasn't time now and there would be plenty of time to pick up the pieces once they left. I'd have all the time in the world. She turned to Willow and held out her hand, Willow watched for a moment, her eyes hard. But the hard look melted away soon enough and she took the hand with a hesitant smile.

Sachiko led the way and Baku was finally so tired of Cole's staring that he changed shape to mirror him. His reaction was even better than when he had seen him as an elephant. He just about choked on air as he gasped. I laughed wholeheartedly and he looked at me, at first a bit miffed then smiling his wide friendly smile, the one that always let me know everything would be fine. I noticed Willow glancing at him and wondered how many times I missed her doing that. Thinking back to the hospital I had seen her watch him there too.

For a moment I wondered if she liked him, but I didn't let the thought linger, it didn't matter either way. He could do much worse than the kind hearted shadow of the forest who helped save him. Cole stumbled and I remembered that he'd just come out of a coma. Looking at Baku, I let my worry show and raised a questioning eyebrow, hoping he would understand.

"You have wanted to see an elephant for so long, Cole, would you like to ride one?" he asked him, still a golden dust mirror of him.

Cole's eyes widened before he smiled widely.

Arro chuckled next to me, patiently tagging along, knowing what was happening. That he and I'd have forever, but Cole and I only had right now. I guess he already understood eternity and had grown more patient than I could hope to be yet. When I looked into Arro's eyes, as Cole made his way to Baku who once again looked like a massive gray elephant, they still held that fire and fervor for me and I smiled widely, this was what I'd have when Cole was gone.

I'd have Arro.

I'd have forever.

I'd be fine... *right?*

I would be just fine...

We walked and as we did, Sachiko spoke to Willow and Kaede. I enjoyed just being around everyone, my eyes lingering on Cole now and then as he rode Baku and watched the scenery with such wonder and awe I couldn't help but realize that with how alike we looked. I must have looked nearly the same when I came here. I couldn't stop smiling seeing him so alive, so happy. I got to do this for him, to bring him here, to make the trade, to help him ride an elephant and give him the freedom he would end up needing when he left here. The freedom to live a life without restraints.

My mind flashed back to the accident. Us lying on the ground just out of reach, the sidewalk painted red with life and death. To the two sided coin we had become that just kept spinning. Spinning. Spinning.

"It'll be okay. You'll be okay." Arro's hand grasped mine firmly as he whispered the words in my ear and it felt like his hand was the only thing keeping me grounded.

I smiled and met his eyes as we continued on, this time when I looked away, it was my turn to catch Cole staring at me.

We passed the forest and then the field, heading the opposite direction of the sanctum. I didn't want them to see the palace, the overly ornate cage. The sky was once again violet as we walked and when I watched Cole, I could tell he slowly tired. I didn't want him to sleep, but I knew it was just my own greed. For the last part of the walk he slept and I watched his peaceful face with the comforting knowledge that while riding on Baku's back there would be no nightmares. The world inside of his mind was his own to create.

I knew we were close when I heard running water, but I still couldn't see it. It still just looked like a forest on one side and an open field on the other. The light here hadn't changed as though sunset were daylight whereas bright sunlight and dark nights were the alluring passing phases. It was funny how perspective could change. I wanted rain, grey skies crying out like my heart. But I wouldn't cause them. I wouldn't allow the same rain that had pelted us on the road as I lay dying to be a part of my last memories with him. My fantasy incarnate.

When I looked back, Willow stared at me, a soft ink tear running down her cheek. She was holding her mother's hand and let it drop softly. Sachiko paused, frightened, but her features smoothed again when she saw Willow walking toward me. I paused, not knowing what to expect as she wrapped her arms around me with so much force I took a step back.

"Thank you," she whispered into my hair and I could feel her tears on my shoulder like a strange transfer of ink only able to pass between two painted girls.

"You were my first true friend. You have given me this time with my mother, in this place she loved that I resented for so long. The place I wanted to belong. I can feel it too, the way this place wraps in on us as though we're a part of it." She was right; through the stag even I could feel her presence here. She belonged here but she didn't, she belonged between worlds when there was no in between, except for when she looked at Cole. When she looked at Cole...

She belonged there; in the other world with him. How long had she known?

We stood there without words as the depth of the situation stood between us. I saved him for me— out of my greed. I couldn't live with the weight of his life on my shoulders, but it hadn't occurred to me just how many people it could affect. I'd always known he would touch lives, he would change things one day, but I hadn't thought about love... that people would love him. That she did. How? They hadn't even had any time? But then...

I looked at Arro and could feel it. This forest. This forest showed you what you wanted without you having to grasp at the muddled straws you had to on the other side, trying to dig for the truth among so many possibilities. This place, it gave even more possibilities, possibilities so endless that you forget to be confused and just know.

I closed my eyes, feeling my emotions boiling over. Feeling the way I always teetered between okay and not okay at all collapsing because she had turned to hug me for a reason. Because she'd figured it out.

She had seen it, she'd seen me.

That maybe something that was a part of Cole had rubbed off. That if this truly were greed I'd have saved him and left letting this radiant world burn and fade.

I'm not invisible anymore.

I closed my eyes and held my breath, praying I wouldn't cry. Praying for strength, asking the stag to hold my heart steady. I could tell my emotions were written across my skin even as I tried to hide them. Even as I looked at Willow and her tears fell, seeing me haunted, seeing what I was giving them all. That I was giving myself and doing so gladly, but it didn't make it hurt less and I both loved and hated it because while it felt like redemption it also felt like death.

Redemption was all I needed. I wanted to be the redeemed, not the lost. Lost forever in a never-ending cycle of self-punishment caused by a low self-worth. The cycle was broken now. Slowly I was healing, becoming more than I allowed myself to be before in my life.

"I will make it worth it. We'll have the most incredible life you can imagine. He will be happy whether with me or someone else. I will make sure of it." She looked into my eyes as she spoke and I believed her. She was telling the truth, I could feel the power of her belief radiating off of her and it helped pull me back together again. I sniffled and looked at Cole who still lay sleeping on Baku's massive back. I smiled at the bittersweet adoration that rose within me.

Willow took my hand and led me back to Sachiko and Kaede who took their cue to keep walking. Arro stayed at my side, following closely, but making sure he was never too close to Sachiko. I asked the stag what Arro was feeling, what he saw when he looked at me and a flash of overwhelming passion ran through me. I miss stepped and almost fell over, but Willow caught me. "You okay?"

"Mmhmm," I answered, knowing the color that showed my emotions this time would have even before my transformation, warmth spreading across my cheeks as I blushed. Joy rose within me at the strength of his emotions. The very person who had taught me 'belief was power' had believed in me. I'd always dreamt of being loved, but I'd promised myself long ago that I'd never marry and risk my mother's fate. This was different. It wasn't just happiness or want. It wasn't cruel or forced, it was just... something else. Something I'd never felt and even now wasn't sure I felt toward him, but... for the first time I wanted to. I wanted to love, the kind of love that consumes you and takes you over.

The kind that makes you want to start again and believe in everything.

I looked over at him and when our eyes met, my blush deepened as I looked away. So many emotions running through me that I thought I might burst and for once, nearly all of them filled with love, longing, and joy. The only thing giving me the bittersweet taste in my mouth was that idea that at the end of the next sunrise Cole would be walking away from me.

But even then...he was alive.

Someone loved him and was going to watch out for him... it all... I was so mixed up I couldn't riddle it out. I was sure my shadows showed it playing across my body, but this time I didn't try to hide it. I'd be okay with who I was.

Me.

My father was wrong about me.

His words were a cruel cover to hide behind.

He was the cold one. He was the bad one. He was the broken one.

Not Me. I wouldn't let it hold me back again, even if it never disappeared. I was happy to be who I was and no one would take that away again. I was the kind of person who would sacrifice, who could love, and who could live even as she died.

What more could I ask of myself?

CHAPTER SEVENTEEN

No wonder this was what Sachiko wanted them to see while we waited for the ceremony, it was magnificent. Willow let go of my hand and looked at Cole. Someone had to wake him up. When she turned back to the view she took in the splendor. I waited. I wanted to feel it at the same time as Cole this time, just this once and one day it could be the place I came to when I thought of him; when I missed my hero. As Baku knelt I glanced at Sachiko, she was so happy. It gave me the strength to smile as I rose to Cole's side and sat, watching him for a moment.

He smiled sweetly even in his sleep and I hoped I'd remember that precious smile. "Cole."

His eyes started to open lazily and when he saw the sky above him he just stared for a moment. I turned my head to look up as well and could see why, it was astonishing and night was coming soon. Deep blues slowly creeping in on the vibrant autumn leaf sky.

"I love it here," he whispered softly and I smiled. "If I ever had to part ways with you, at least I go knowing I'm leaving you in the most extraordinary place I've ever seen. Somewhere filled with wonder, somewhere like the worlds we once talked about when we sat by the graves. Somewhere that makes me feel... like you are safe. Like you will always be loved."

I couldn't hold it back now. I could feel the shadows on my face, clouding around my eyes. I took his hand and he sat up, watching me and then smiling ever so softly. A smile that made me want to cry because it wasn't filled with joy, soft and fragile; a smile both resigned and sad. I could feel the stag speak to me, telling me things I needed to hear, but most of all telling me what Cole needed to hear; giving me the gift of being the one to say the words.

"The forest will always be a part of you, Cole. Your heart was a part of this place and that means you and me, we are still a part of each other. We always have been and always will be and one day when fate is kinder we will be together again. When fate pulls the strings of our lives close again. Who knows how many times each of us has met. How much history we may still have buried between us. You and I. The connection we have is forever and every time you speak to me you will be able to hear my whispered reply. We will still be together, always. Just as we always were."

"You don't understand. I drove. This is my fault. The crash, our lives. I was the one who was supposed to save you." He started to feel it all again like he had at the crash site. It made me feel distant from him, but closer at the same time. I'd seen him break, but hadn't realized how much I could break him. What losing me could do to him.

"No you weren't," I said, strength rising up to meet the sadness. "You weren't meant to save me and you never hurt me. We were meant to save each other. And we have. You gave this to me." I raised my hands and motioned the world around us. "You have given me the most precious of gifts. Everything I am is in part thanks to you and from here, I can do good. I can help, like you always wanted to and somewhere deep inside, I think I did too."

"I know, Lily, but…"

I saw it in his eyes. He didn't want to leave me. He felt the same way I had watching him slowly die only I stood right here, staring into his eyes.

"I know," I said, "I know. I will miss you too. Even when I speak to you, even when I hear your words, I've always been so accustomed to having you by my side…but Cole? We don't have long. Let me show you this place now, while I can. We will have all the time in the world to feel our loss, but let's wait until it has happened. Let's promise to make the rest of our time together as happy and beautiful as we can. Let's give ourselves something precious to hold on to when we think of each other. Be strong for me one last time."

He smiled at me. "So strong." He messed up my hair.

"Oh blah," I responded and hopped down then raised a hand up so that I could try to steady him even though I was fairly certain it wouldn't work with the drop.

He dropped and teetered for a moment before he regained his balance and turned to Baku, "Thank you, friend."

Baku bowed his head and I could see the twinkle in his eyes. The sandman, so attached to everything and everyone that their joy was his own and their nightmares his own too. I wondered what his story held, how he'd come to be here in this strange place filled with so much beauty.

Cole and I walked toward the incredible sight of the waterfall, his arm bent so that mine could wrap through it at our sides. We used to walk this way to and from school, sometimes skipping and sometimes just silent, not caring if anyone judged because they always had and nothing we could do would stop them. Though he'd always been better at thinking that way than I. I'd still worry even when he didn't seem to have a care in the world, like he'd been untouchable.

A bridge stood in front of us stretching across a deep gorge that plunged so far down you couldn't see the bottom, only darkness. The waterfall above flowing down into the endless abyss. The sound oddly striking. I'd never heard a waterfall before. It sounded like waves crashing, but thousands all at once without end. The bridge was made of the same living red wood the palace had been, as wide as a two lane road, probably to accommodate spirits like Baku and the dragon.

"If you stay here long enough there are spirits that like to dive off of it. Koichi is one of them. Don't let it startle you though, she is a water spirit, the fall doesn't cause her any harm. She once told me that it made her feel more alive, more whole as though she were about to be a part of something larger than she'd ever known." Sachiko smiled.

Willow and Kaede looked on in wonder and I knew I cherished this moment too, that this, all of this would be important to me. Even Kaede's wide smile and Baku lazily lying in the grass in a pose that resembled a dog or cat more than an ancient majestic elephant.

Cole smiled too, listening to Sachiko in awe and wrapping his arm around me every few moments as though making sure I hadn't drifted away from him or slipped over the side. For a moment I just let the beauty wash over me, soaking it all in. The sounds, the smiles, the feel of Cole's arm around my shoulders and Arro's hand in mine. This would console my heart when it felt like that waterfall, tremendous waves falling into nothingness. One day they would come back to me. Each of them belonged here in their own way. Each of them belonged with me.

Then a feeling washed over me so forcefully I stood perfectly still. Not the kind that causes you to fall to your knees or think softer thoughts, but the kind that hits you with so much force your body can't keep up or react. You stand there star struck and physically unmoved, but emotionally changed. My mind raced and I tried to fight it with everything I had. I stood there and saw two scenes in front of me. One of the people I loved laughing and smiling and another of the bridge we stood on crumbling beneath us and dropping out from under us.

Another where I had caused it all. Where I'd caused pain. I couldn't cause any more pain. I'd done enough, hadn't I? But I was about to do more. I was about to do worse and I could feel it in every inch of me. I could hear glass and sirens. I could hear shouting and crying and a steady rhythm like a heartbeat pulsing on into eternity. It was me and it wasn't me and it shattered everything inside of me for a moment until I wasn't seeing the world in front of me in all of its promised beauty, but some small piece of the world I had left behind.

I shut it out.

I let it all go and tried to see Arro again. Tried to return to myself, unsure what was happening and not sure that I cared as long as I could get away from it.

When the vision cleared and I was back on the bridge I gasped and choked as the shock of my own happiness seeing everyone there. For a moment my eyes wouldn't work properly, like this were a mirage shifting in and out of focus. Then it cleared and I was firmly back. I was safe. I was loved. I could feel Cole's arms around me and Arro whispering in my ear. As I looked around, I knew I'd collapsed.

Standing again, I brushed myself off even though I knew nothing clung to my clothes, I was brushing at emotions that weren't leaving me. Emotions I didn't want to feel.

You have no choice in this, something deep inside of me said. *You can't go back. Don't fight it.*

I didn't know what it meant, but when I saw my worried loved ones I didn't care quite so much. We walked again, but Arro stayed closer to my side and Cole was ever watchful. His hand resting on mine or his palm against the spot between my shoulder blades as though touching me reassured him, or maybe the other way around.

I had it all.

I was getting everything I'd ever wanted and was learning to heal, so why did something feel so strange? So...

The thought left me by the time we moved on and started walking to see the graves crack. I could hardly wait for Cole to see it. The majestic beauty I wanted so desperately to share with him when I first saw it.

"We're here," Baku said when we arrived and I had a feeling it meant more than I knew. The sky was already turning dark and I watched Cole staring at the vibrant aurora. I watched as each star welcomed into the sky showered his face with flashing lights and even as the thunder sounded, loud overbearing sounds that were familiar somehow, I didn't let my gaze waver.

While looking at the graves he whispered softly, "Kind of reminds you of the graveyard back home, doesn't it?" and I smiled, finally looking away. I watched the graves appear and leave and knew it similar to life itself. That I'd seen hummingbirds and pitied their short life spans, but in the scope of reality every lifespan was a flash of lighting or a roar of thunder.

I remembered my parent's graves and said my own silent apology to my mother for the turns her life had taken. I could accept what she had done now; it wouldn't break me though it still hurt. I wondered if Cole knew. If he had accepted it yet. That she had broken the shattered pieces left of her soul for us in one final act. That she had tried to bring back the man she loved and since she couldn't she couldn't let him come back to hurt us again.

The truth was, the town thought we had killed our parents or that we were the poor orphans to be pitied, but in reality, our mother had done the one thing she could to protect us. She had taken it upon herself to ensure our father could never hurt us again. The police had known, but they wouldn't reveal it to the public out of kindness to us, the plus side of a small town was the same as the downside.

We'd cried so desperately when we'd found out, but more than anything we were confused. At first they thought our parents were mugged, but the truth was that our father couldn't even be that boy he'd been for long enough to sleep outside in the rain for one night. They couldn't spend one day pretending. Instead they destroyed each other. It was too hard to face, too hard to understand at first, but now, I forgave her. I might never forgive him, but I could forgive her.

I realized someone didn't have to be perfect to be forgivable. She was never meant to do everything right. Cole would live on and he would mess up and he would pick up the pieces and keep going. Just like me. I don't know if I made the right choice, but it was still the choice I made and I'd live with the consequences. I'd hate myself, love myself, and forgive myself. It would all come full circle eventually and if Cole was touched by the forest he would return one day too.

As the last grave crumbled into dust and rose into the sky, flashing brightly and filling the last bit of blue with a flurry of stars we watched in wonder, letting the moment settle into our bones.

"I love you," I said, but I wasn't even sure who to. I meant it to everyone around me; I meant it to my mother and the world here. I just loved too much not to say the words. Hands clasped each of mine and Sachiko watched me, a question written across her skin, ink now unnecessary. She was right, time moved faster and the forest was slowly aching to fight against their presence.

CHAPTER EIGHTEEN

My skin must have painted the picture I could not put words to. I could feel the darkness crawling, my heart on my sleeve just as it'd always been in one form or another, even if it had taken nearly dying to realize it. The darkness changed and though I could feel it deepen the strips of color found their way across and left just as quickly– my own personal aurora borealis. For a moment even I paused to look. Unsettled seeing my emotions painted in such clarity.

Sachiko watched me and I knew, she'd realized what spurred my emotions. "Let's start toward the pathway. We don't want to stray too far."

She watched me with her dark eyes, her porcelain skin no longer able to reveal her secrets. Arro must've sensed something I didn't, because he backed away from us, moving quickly to Baku's side. I felt his absence like an injury, almost annoyed he'd left my side so willingly. When Sachiko took her hand in mine, holding it between her own and studying it, I understood. He didn't need colors to cross her skin to read her emotions. Something about how similar they were still remained even after everything that had passed.

"It's strange seeing you this way. There are no mirrors here, I don't know if I looked like you do, but it suits you. My hands... they were never like this. So... deeply striking. You feel so much for someone so young." Her voice held a pity I didn't want. It only made the future sneaking up on us one heartbeat at a time that much more real. I looked at anything but her as she continued to hold my hand, turning it this way and that. The sky changing again, the colors still tinted with violet like they'd been when I first went to meet Cole on the bridge.

"Thank you?" I said, not sure what else to say to fill the silence. To be honest, I didn't want to admit the depths of what I'd done or the repercussions. I wouldn't let her make me face them until I needed to.

"I was young too," she whispered softly, the subject shifting to one I felt more comfortable with, even if it pained her.

"You still are," I said, hoping it held true. Her body was young, younger than Kaede by nearly a decade. It didn't seem to matter seeing them next to one another, but it still struck me.

"No, not in the way that counts." Her hand brushed against her chest, the spot just over her heart. The kimono still striking. I'd almost forgotten how foreign she'd felt to me even hours ago. Now, I was the foreign one, somehow we'd switched worlds. She belonged to mine and I to hers, but I wondered how much either of us would ever really belong anywhere.

"Have you really changed so much?" It was my turn to look at my hands as Sachiko dropped them. She looked from my own hands to hers and back again.

"I don't know. Not anymore. I just want...want. I don't know the words. It's like I could drown in the possibilities and I need to take each one and hold it close to me. I don't want to pick. I want it all. I sound like I'm filled with greed and maybe I am. After all, I let you take my place so I could escape. What kind of woman does that?"

"Maybe a woman doesn't," I said before I could stop myself. I only realized how it sounded when it was too late. "I just mean..." I didn't know how to say it.

"Maybe it's the kind of thing a girl does?" Sachiko asked, humor in her eyes.

I should have realized she'd forgive me anything in exchange for her freedom. Of course she was right, it was what I'd meant.

"You were a child when you came here, but does age really matter anymore? Do titles? You've been a woman, a girl, a child, a leader, the voice, a shadow, and who knows what else. You're allowed to be emotional, you're allowed to..." Saying the words I realized I needed to hear them.

"It wasn't your fault you know..."

"What?" I stepped away from her so quickly Baku and Arro turned toward us.

"Whatever happened to you. It wasn't your fault. Like the fire that brought me here. I couldn't stop it and as much as I hate to admit it... neither could he."

She wasn't even crying, but her emotions held more force than a thousand tears. For the first time the sky here did not tinged violet, but red. I couldn't see or think straight, the world crumbled beneath me, but it didn't. There was a cacophony of sounds from chimes to sirens in my mind and none of it mattered.

I was alone, but I'd never be alone again.

My hand went to my heart and I could feel the hart's emotions connected to my own. I could feel the stability he radiated, the way everything inside of him was in a constant state of being both ancient and new. I let him calm me, taking more of me than felt comfortable. The sky turned violet again when I opened my eyes, but the words remained, sitting deep inside of me– unmoving.

"You've done good here," she whispered as we started moving again.

Just like you always wanted to, the forest whispered inside of me, filling me with warmth I wasn't sure I deserved.

I smiled softly and moved to Cole's side. He'd taught me how. His trade was intended to free me and it had. His warmth radiated out from him, but as I touched his hand for the barest of instances I thought I'd touched thin air. Even with my newfound grace my aim was atrocious. I reached again and found him, his touch just as I'd always remembered it. At one point Willow reached for his other hand and my insides squirmed with delight. I'd never seen him so shy and something about it was absolutely wonderful. We walked slowly, taking in every leaf on the wind and even a few whirring humming bird like spirits that whizzed past us and toward the entrance.

"Can they cross over?" I asked aloud wondering if anyone might know the answer.

"Hummingbirds are strange creatures," Baku said, taking on Kaede's form and imitating him with such intensity that Cole put his arm around Willow to stop her from falling over as her whole body shook with laughter.

I'd never been so happy.

The walk was a luxury. Moments of pure bliss collecting around us as we enjoyed the simplest of pleasures– each other's company. Before we knew it the day had passed us by and sunset followed across our path, creeping ever closer. My skin reacted, writhing as time fled from us too quickly. I felt Cole start to grow weak, but I held on with everything I was. Everything I knew him to be. He needed to leave and I needed to let him go. As we walked, I wondered if I could. His first steps back into our world felt like they'd be walking right over my heart.

Sachiko was all too aware of the time. She wouldn't risk her loved ones. Even her greed could not keep her from what she wanted. She would have it all and I would have...

I wasn't sure. It felt like I had it all now, but it also felt unreal, not quite the way it should be. When Kaede coughed roughly, the spell broke. We were still too far from the gate and the sunset was catching up with us. Kaede and Cole were feeling its affects.

"We need to go," Sachiko ordered.

"Not yet, they have a bit longer," I said, but when she turned to me I knew I was the one being greedy now. I couldn't endanger them for a few stolen moments.

Cole looked at me like he had so many times before and we felt right in each other's company, we didn't need precedence or even words. We stood there like that, silently watching one another and I knew I would miss his companionship more than anything. I didn't need the outside world, but somehow, I still needed him, even if I didn't... I just did. The kind of need that was chosen and more powerful for it.

"Go..." I said softly thinking maybe I could stay behind and let them leave me here; that I might spare myself seeing him take those last steps so I could imagine he was still here with me forever.

It is time to let go. I could hear the hart whisper to me, filling me with the ticking of the clock until it was all I could hear.

Then Cole spoke, "There is no way I can stay?"

"No." Saying the word made it true.

Only Cole's safely crossing mattered now, and if he didn't run soon he might never make it. The last thing I wanted was for him to die here. I wasn't even sure what might happen, but what I felt from the hart scared me, legends of revenge and pain from those who'd been caught in between worlds lingered between us in our connection.

"I did this so that you could live the life we always wanted. Live it for the both of us. It'll hurt, we both know it will hurt being apart, but it won't be forever. Remember what you always said when we would watch those silly movies?"

"There is no such thing as eternity," he said the words, but his voice rang hollow, he didn't believe it anymore, now he'd seen the proof. He knew better. "It's different now."

"No, it really isn't, but it means us being apart isn't eternal either," I said softly, hearing the light chimes in the air again, but this time they were faint, nearly fading. "Cole, I know you gave me a gift, but in the end the choice is mine. Maybe you can change fate, but think of what I've already gotten from your gift. Think of everything you can still have out there. Isn't that still what you want?"

"Yes," he admitted.

The ticking inside of me drove me toward panic. Everything was crashing inwards and I didn't want him to be a casualty of my journey.

"Then it's time you get to live. Really truly live. Leave everything behind and dream those wonderful crazy dreams you've always been so full of. You were meant to do something and so am I. I'm doing it now. You need to let go just for now so that I'll be able to. So that I can find peace here, and have everything we never had before. We will both be living out our dreams."

"But not together."

"Cole, we are always together," I said, laying my hand on his chest. "Please, you have to go. You have to run."

"I won't leave you here."

The words cut through me as I turned away from him. This time

I needed to be the strong one, to show him the truth even when he couldn't see what was right in front of him. Time was running out and when Sachiko looked at me I nodded. They had to go or we were risking too much. She managed to get Kaede to start running without her, knowing she would follow, but Willow wouldn't leave Cole.

"Why should I go if you stay? Why can't I just become whatever it is you have become? Then we can be together. Here, in this unforgettable place, forever."

I wanted to tell him he could stay and we had forever to learn and grow together; that he could be here, ageless for as long as he wanted. Yet, even as we stood there, I could feel the forest rejecting him against my will, pulling us away from each other. I knew it was only a matter of time before it would inflict on him the pain that already started burrowing its way through my chest.

In a startling moment of clarity, I realized the scene before me reflected Sachiko and Arro's story. The sunset blazed forest and the entrance his only escape from my pulling him under.

"I wish you could," I whispered, but I hoped he hadn't heard.

He needed to let go. It would only hurt him worse knowing I wanted him by my side just as badly as he wished to stay, because it would mean this chance was being taken from both of us. I didn't know what to say for a moment as I watched him. The sun burned brighter, my own emotions and the imagery running through my mind changing the colors of the world around us.

I knew he felt the pain by now, he must have known he didn't belong. He had a life just as wondrous as this place ahead of him, love and vitality in his reality. I had here. The truth was, for a moment, I wanted to be by his side, but I just couldn't leave.

The sky turned into a tumultuous storm, I couldn't keep holding on to the past, but I just couldn't let go and somehow Cole was the conduit at the center of it all, the grand symbol of everything that ever had or ever could have been. Everything I would be losing by staying here. The chimes sounded again, the ticking in my head now a pulsing so loud I was terrified it might shake the ground between us. He needed to stay on his feet. He needed to be strong and run like Sachiko and Arro had... like I would in his place.

But he wasn't moving.

He couldn't be a coward, even for me.

Therein lay the difference between us. Even Willow backed away from the sky behind me, the burning clouds scaring her away. Kaede crossed the bridge with Sachiko, calling out to Willow wildly, but she kept her eyes on Cole, his face lit by the light. I couldn't help but feel a penetrating horror at the thought of him burning like Sachiko almost had. So many people had lost so much. Was I really giving up so much more just by letting him live the life he'd always deserved?

"RUN!" I screamed, I couldn't contain it anymore. The panic eating me away. I'd do anything to save him. "Run, GO!"

"No..." he said, standing firm even as he started to crumple under the pain, my own eyesight going blurry and spinning as I tried to let him go, trying to hold the forest at bay.

Willow held her hand out toward Cole.

"Go. I'm happy here." I didn't feel happy, I felt like I was ripping out my own heart. Like I was the one doing this to me and not fate. This forest always seemed to ask someone to be away from the one they loved. It asked Sachiko the same after she found Kaede, and now it was my turn. Staying wasn't my price, this was. "I traded places so that you could live out there, so that you could have the life you were meant to have. I can't be what takes you away from that. You deserve to see the good you always believed in."

"But Lily..."

"No. No, buts. Go. Please. I will always be with you, but you are running out of time. I don't want to hurt you." I moved toward him, shoving him hard in the direction of the bridge, but though he stumbled he didn't give in. "Please!" I screamed and kept pushing him back step by step toward Willow. I didn't want to hurt him, I didn't want to be the one to push, but I couldn't let him stay. I couldn't let my past continue to...

"No." He stood strong, his eyes going cold with the challenge he knew he posed. The edges of his face were burning red, the legs of his pants darkening, like he were a picture being lit on fire and I was helpless to do anything again. Just as helpless as I'd always been. I didn't know how he withstood it. "I won't leave you. If I can't stay here, then you come with me. Come and have the life you always deserved. I'll make sure you get anything and everything you ever wanted."

"Cole... Please..."

"I will be there and make sure no one hurts you again. I will protect you, and this time it will be different. The way it's meant to be. We can be together. We wanted that life. Not you, not me... us. It was always meant to be the two of us. I can make it happen, I don't know how yet, but Lily, I promise I can. You're my sister. My twin. How can you expect me to desert you like everyone else deserted us? Is that really how you see me? Like one of them?"

"Cole!" I raise my voice, I could feel the pain, but by now his pain would be worse than mine. He was burning. He wasn't like us, Sachiko,

Arro and I... he didn't have our strength to run. Our sense of self pres-ervation. Willow ran to him, trying to lift him.

"No! I won't go! Stop it!" He shook her off.

"Cole..." Arro was at my side as I cried. He held me back. "What do I..."

The thought occurred to me. I felt shame for thinking of it. I was go-ing to inflict on him the very thing I'd barely forgiven him for inflicting on me. I was going to act this time. I would be the hero.

A pact.

He wouldn't feel this pain if he left. He would never feel losing me if I never existed to him. He didn't need this. He could walk away from this and into a new life without our past, without the crash.

No, I couldn't do such a thing.

A lie.

I could. It was the selfish part of me that didn't want this, that wanted him to remember me, to love me. I needed his love. I always had and in that moment, I knew I always would.

"Arro," I cried softly and he wrapped his arms around me, "I'm sor-ry for asking, but I can't watch him die, not after all of this. Not here."

"What is it?" he asked, his voice tender.

I knew he would do it, but still... I didn't want to ask. I couldn't hes-itate. He was burning... He was burning and I...

"Can you... take his memories of me?" I almost stopped breathing as the words left my mouth. I could only exhale and the tears flowed in a stream so steady and fierce I couldn't see through them. "He... I..."

I couldn't. I couldn't. I felt like I drowned, all I could see was a blur of Arro as he held me and we moved toward Cole.

"What are you doing?" Cole said, his voice weak.

I begged the stag for strength; just enough, just barely enough and I could do this.

"I'm sorry, Cole. Truly." I could hear Arro's voice, but I still couldn't see and I didn't want to. I didn't want to see the moment my brother, my twin, would become something other than my brother. Someone who wouldn't know me better than anyone else in the world ever had, or ever could. Someone who had always been a part of everything I had ever been or wanted to be. It felt like a part of me was dying knowing he would never look at me the same way again, knowing that now I would hear his prayers, but he might never again say my name or... What choice did I have?

Was this what it felt like to be a hero?

I fell to the ground as the rain start to fall, the forest crying with me and shielding Cole from the fire for a few moments longer. Through the stag's eyes, I could see the scene. He allowed me this one last glimpse of Cole that I was too weak to give myself. He was so...everything. Had Cole always been this way? Had he always been so integral?

I watched as the pact was made, Arro in his true form.

A parallel to the crash site, only I was the one changing our fate.

"What are you doing?" This time it was Willow. Her voice was concerned, as though Arro were wasting precious time, not simply throwing Cole over his back. No, it had to be this way. It just had to. I wasn't sure how I knew, but I had to sacrifice to stay here and he had to let go to move on.

"If he doesn't leave, he dies. She is giving up yet another thing to save him. To save you." Arro looked into Cole's eyes, his words now directed at him. I could see the panic in Cole's features, he didn't understand. He couldn't comprehend what Arro said and I knew Willow hadn't figured it out yet. As the rain sheltered them, the fire stormed under my skin. Ink flames burning me whole, but I couldn't stop the tears or the way my breathing seemed to shock in and out of me so unnaturally.

My body didn't want to breathe through so much pain, it didn't want anything anymore. I was soaking the people I loved in my tears to try and stop them from burning alive, but I could see the realization as Cole thought he was dying, then realized something else happened instead. Arro stared deep into Cole's eyes, his fur flat against him, already soaked through. He touched his nose to Cole's and when he backed away, I forced my hands into my mouth to stifle the part of me that wanted to scream. The part of me that wanted to cry out to stop him even though he had seconds left. He had to cross the bridge. I looked at Willow, my eyes pleading as much as they could though I still couldn't let myself see the truth. I asked the stag to let me see him go, to let me watch him get across safely.

"Hurry!" Arro yelled at a shell-shocked Willow who still didn't realized what I'd done, though Cole stared around blankly.

Without the memories of me, the fire struck terror into his heart and he turned. She didn't know how much I'd betrayed everything just to fix everything. What I gave him. What I took from myself. He was the last part of me that was human, the last part of me that belonged on the other side of that bridge.

Willow ushered Cole across, practically carrying him and not easily at that. He was safe... He was safe...

He was safe...

Arro rushed to my side, he'd come to me when I needed him most, but now I needed something else. My last view of Cole gone... hardly an image at all. Arro cradled me in his arms, his hold on me fierce and

SHADOWS OF THE FOREST

full of emotion. As though seeing me so broken hurt him. Maybe it did. *What had I done?*

Then the stag's vision reappeared. I could see Cole, Willow, Kaede and Sachiko running toward a large gate. I remembered when I'd first come here, the rules. Kaede had said I was only able to leave through the gates he'd taken us through to get to the hospital. I watched them, memorizing everything I could and wondering if one day I might walk out of those gates too and find him again.

Goodbye, Cole. I love you. You may not remember me, but I'll always remember you. Until the day I die, until this forest turns cold and gray. You are loved. You will always be loved, I promised myself.

He looked so familiar to me. So... home.

Yes, our eyes were similar, same color, same shape and even our long dark lashes practically matched, but his were full of everything I always needed, strength, love, and hope. I felt like I was losing all of that as he walked through the overbearing gates. They were strange, the two sides of the gates not matching one another; one a deep black, swirling and ornate, the other white and made of straight barred iron. I couldn't see his face. As they walked out, Willow turned to close the gates behind them. I could see her scanning the tree line for any signs of life. Her eyes met the stag and she called out to him. "One day we will find a way back. We will see you again, I promise, this isn't the end."

Then I understood why they'd run. The hospital was in chaos and the sky looked almost as though my fiery storm had somehow seeped through the entry. Chasing them even once they'd thought they were free. Then I realized what she'd said...

They'd come back.

I felt hope rising back to the surface in my heart, even as they left my

148

side, even though the pain left me laying on the forest's floor, clinging to the stability as night fell around me. My beautiful night. They left the stag's sight just beyond the gates and my vision became my own again. For a moment I thought I saw something strange, but I could feel the stag embracing my heart, comforting me in every way he could. Filling me with the knowledge that I still had hope, love, kindness, strength and each of the things I'd treasured in my other half. Just because we felt like halves of each other didn't mean we were. We could both be strong. We could both be brave and with the help of this world and time to heal, we could both be whole.

CHAPTER NINETEEN

I could feel Arro turn into a fox, his arms around me loosening as he backed away to shift. I questioned his actions, but the stag gave me the answer.

His emotions; they'd overcome his human form. They were too overwhelming and his original form, as he's proclaimed so many times, is the fox.

The effort to be human was normally so minimal it was nearly non-existent, until the emotions in him matched the sorrow he felt at having passed. The sorrow after he was captured. He curled his form around me and I draped my body over his soft fur, melting into his comfort just as a young Sachiko had with the stag when she left her old life behind. *I will only allow myself to grieve now.*

Only tonight.

Tomorrow will be kinder.

Tomorrow I will be stronger.

I can live without him.

I. Just. Need. Tonight.

I wept for my brother, for myself, for our family that had gone anything but according to plan. For Sachiko's village and Arro's guilt. I wept for all the times I'd wanted to, but was too afraid to let the cracks in my cold exterior show. Terrified that if I started I might never stop. I thought about everything and nothing. An oblivion that I'd only let consume me for this one precious night.

I cried knowing I left Cole behind, but I cried harder knowing I wanted this, knowing that some part of me I didn't want to acknowledge needed this. Needed to be here. Here. Here. Here.

Here.

I thought of the crash. I remembered the glass, the sounds of shards falling like rain as I moved so quickly it felt like time itself was abrasive.

Then I saw it. The crash. Cole. All of it. Connected and disconnected. It was all...

Like a puzzle that sat there, waiting to be seen and rearranged.

I was wrong. I died. I was...

Dead.

"I think we're lost," cautioned Cole's voice apologetic.

We'd spent so long staring at the map; I couldn't blame him for having forgotten to check it the last few turns. We probably both had the route memorized from our bug-out plans.

"No worries, I'll grab the map."

"No, Lily. UGTH!"

I could tell he was annoyed, as I took off my seatbelt to reach into the back seat, but we needed the map and it would only take a second. Hardly even that. I'd just grab it and snap the seat belt right back on.

I reached into the backseat, but I couldn't quiet grab the map. I lifted my leg to get a better hold over the center divider and just managed to grasp it. I sat back down and smiled at Cole. "See, easy-peasy."

I flipped it open and traced my finger along the familiar route. We planned this trip for so long. We had wanted to go the second we'd turned sixteen and we nearly had. We'd decided to think of this as our birthday present to ourselves. Finally getting away.

I lowered the map and thought back to the turns we'd taken. It didn't seem like anything was off. It was just a longer road than it looked like on the map. As used to looking at this thing as we were, it wasn't like that gave us any idea of the actual time it took to cross the landscapes.

"Nah, we're all good. Just keep going straight."

"It's so green here. So beautiful."

"Meh, forests," I grumbled. Our parent's only semi-mysterious death had taken place in a forest and somehow when I looked at them I was still terrified my father might be lurking, concealed by their foliage, waiting for me.

Cole laughed, light heartedly. "Don't be so hard on the forest, it couldn't control who went into it."

"If only it could have. Sure would've saved a lot of trouble. If a forest knew who should get to stay or go and would clear a path for those that deserved one. Hah, bastard would've gotten caught in so many brambles. Forest really would have killed him instead of…"

"Hey, it isn't as black and white as all of that."

"I know…" I wanted to argue, but he was right. There was nothing black and white about any of this. The only reason their entire town didn't know the true cause of death was because of the sheriff. Still…we knew what she'd done and why I'd rather blame a forest than the person responsible.

"Do you think…" I said the words without meaning to. No, that's a lie. I did mean to, but I knew I shouldn't. I didn't want to know. Not really. I don't think either of us did.

"That she did it for us, you mean?" he continued and I became acutely aware of the fact that he simply knew me too well for me to hide the majority of my thoughts from him. "Yeah, I think she did. She told me she was going out there to see if he was still the man she'd married. I think when she realized he wasn't, when she saw that he might never be again... I don't know. Sometimes it's hard to see options. Maybe she thought it was the only way." Cole had always known and understood more than I.

"I can't imagine him any different than...well, how he was to us."

"No one starts out that way. No one." He peered ahead as though trying to see something in the distance, but then shook it off and kept talking. "So, what should we do first when we get there?"

"Uhhhhh, find an apartment?" I asked, but I was chuckling. I didn't care what we did first. I liked the idea of going to some weird restaurant and sharing a piece of pie to celebrate, but I wasn't even sure how much money we had to our name. Cole was in charge of that kind of thing, the responsible one.

"Oh come on! We've gotta celebrate!" he said, his voice full of excitement and joy.

"Pie?" I asked and he smiled.

"Perfect! We'll have pie. It's a big city, maybe they'll have a kind we didn't get to try at Maa's Shoppe."

"Mmmmmm... like blueberry?" I asked. Maa was allergic to blueberries so she wasn't about to let anyone else on the planet get to eat any of them if she could help it.

"Ohhhh. Yeah," he said, as though he were so hungry he was ready to sit down and eat an entire one. I laughed. He was always hungry even though he couldn't gain weight if he tried. Damn metabolism.

"Hey, do you see that?" His voice wavered like he needed the reassuring gesture of saying I had, but the truth was I wasn't even looking at the road. "I thought I saw..."

Something large and white ran out into the road in front of us, too close for the car to stop in time.

A white deer.

Shit.

Seatbelt.

It's strange the way thoughts change when something catastrophic happens. I could only think in simple statements for a moment. I worried about Cole. I thought about Mom. I wondered why I'd forgotten to re-buckle the seatbelt. Stupid thoughts. Inconsequential notions that for a moment stalled my brain from realizing I was about to catapult forward and the car had started to skid out of control.

I could feel so much and so little. It was like nothing I'd felt before. Terrifying and a thousand times worse than any vertigo. Almost like the fact that I was moving forward couldn't even occur to me yet, but my body couldn't block the fear, the physical knowledge that this wasn't natural, this wasn't right. Then the glass shattered and for a moment that was all I could feel. I was flying, but my body was contorting until it felt like I was flying backwards, but my back was against asphalt. Asphalt. Was I moving?

I couldn't tell anymore.

I'd been thrown from the car.

Like a delayed reaction, I felt the overwhelming impact before I went spinning. I could still hear glass. Like wind chimes, but each clatter, each crash was fracturing. Like an avalanche that started with a few pieces that somewhere along the way, had become so many they were everywhere. When I managed to see, even though my eyes had never closed, all I could see was the stag and my blood pooling next to my face. And I knew. I was leaving this place. I was dying. I was going and there was nothing I could do about it.

As though my body was bidding me a sad farewell, filling me with a knowledge that consumed me. I still stared at the stag we hadn't meant to take from this world, I saw that Cole's airbag had gone off. He was inside. His seatbelt was fastened as always. He would be safe. I on the other hand...

I wasn't.

I managed to move my head, a light roll that sent shockwaves of pain through my body, but left me staring out into the forest. My blood was pooling around me heavily now, mixing with the stag's. I wouldn't look at myself. I didn't want to see. How could I have been so damn stupid? What had I done? All of this thanks to a seatbelt, thanks to...what did this? Why was everything this way? Why was life like this? I couldn't leave now. I hadn't learned yet, I hadn't seen things or grown or lived or loved or had my first kiss.

If only...

If only a forest really could choose.

If only this forest would save me.

If only I could love, just once, and feel love's tender kiss.

If only I could heal my fractured soul before going to wherever it was people went after this.

I hadn't realized how badly I wanted it all. How badly I wanted everything and if I got through this I'd remember. It was the most important part of me and I hadn't even been able to see it. Why hadn't I seen it? I thought back to my beloved books. Fantasy, history, and especially travel. I wanted to see the world, go to Asia and learn another language. I wanted to see the imperial palace and ride an elephant in India. I wanted to live.

In that moment I wanted to live more than I had ever wanted anything.

But it was too late.

What had I done?

Save me.

"I don't understand," I told Arro who looked at me with his fox eyes and just watched me. Why did the stag let me remember? Why had he let me know this place... "Is this place real?"

He nodded.

What does real even mean though. I wasn't sure I knew. I wasn't sure I cared.

"Cole?"

He shrugged his fox shoulders and when I stood he did too. I wanted to go to the graveyard, the place I'd first seen the stag. There was only one thing I needed to know. The rest would come with time, but... I needed to know if that meant Cole had come here. Or if... It was my way of saying goodbye. To my old life, to who I could have been.

It didn't take us long and as we passed the violet trees, each of them pulled toward me, reaching out to me. Wanting to lend me their comfort. Had I created this place? No. I couldn't have. I didn't have the imagination or heart for it. But how? Had it been here all along? A pocket realm as Arro had called it? The place Kaede once called here when he unintentionally reached out to Usagi?

The hart stood there, majestic as the aurora flew across the sky, wavering its unending light above our heads. Was it still night? Had this all happened so fast or had my first day here without him already passed? I couldn't tell. I wasn't sure how time had moved. It was all so strange and foreign to me suddenly. "I need to know. Is Cole alright?"

Yes.

CHAPTER TWENTY

I awoke in a sunlit field and for a moment the sky belonged to me. Even though only Arro was here, I knew Baku had been for I didn't have memory of nightmares. I hadn't dreamt. Maybe that was what my good dreams would be for now. I looked around, startled into a moment of wonder as I looked at Arro. Something about seeing him this way took my breath away. He didn't feel my gaze, and in that small moment I could see a glimpse of who he might be if his guard were down completely. Someone filled with life when the whole world only knew him for having died. Even in this field with all of its yellows, purples, and gold he was the brightest light and the most beautiful sight.

It was tragic. That something so bright could only be remembered as an act he had no say in committing. Underneath it all was a flawed being, someone who felt real in an 'unreal' world. The sky was too bright, the scenes were almost too majestic, but he was truth. I wanted to know him better and for just a moment, felt like it might be okay. No, I wasn't sure if this place was real, but I wasn't sure I minded that. I needed this place as much as it claimed to need me. I wanted to get to see and understand and maybe in doing so, not so much find myself, as build myself.

As I bolted upright I realized I could choose now.

I could be whoever I wanted to be and in that moment, I understood what true power was. Choice. Not the big neon signs kind of choices like having kids or becoming a doctor, but the quiet choices you make when no one is watching, the studying for that test to get to your next class on that path or saving up for that child's college fund one paycheck at a time for years.

Choices that truly make you who you are when everything else falls away.

And I knew. I knew exactly who that girl was and what she was like. I wasn't there yet, but I could see her in my mind and knew that could be me. I'd keep this forest alive. Keep these ethereal sunrises rising and the crazy nighttime rituals with their glory. I'd watch the souls become stars and answer prayers to the best of my abilities. I could help here. I'd always wanted to be a girl who helped.

It's amazing who you can become once you have truly set your mind on being that person.

The act of deciding empowers. I looked at Arro who saw me this time and smiled, his face full of warmth, but not all traces of that trickster grin gone. He was still the boy I'd met at the hospital and in many ways, I was still that girl. But we'd both changed. We were more now. And somehow, that filled me with excitement. Yes, Cole was away from me, but I'd hold on to Willow's promise and listen to the whispers on the wind. We'd meet again and I wanted him to be proud of who I'd become.

I loved this place and for the first time I realized, I kind of loved me.

What the forest taught me...

1. Healing isn't easy or it wouldn't hurt to break.
2. Your family are the people who accept you. No judgement. They see and love you for everything you are. The flaws, pain, laughter, and smiles are a package deal.
3. Some rules are meant to be broken.
4. Most importantly, it is all worth it.
Every. Last. Breath.

CHAPTER TWENTY ONE

I knew what I wanted to hear. My stones, conduits for communication across the passes I could not cross. I'd become a part of my world and its vast expanse. I helped those who prayed and those who the hart led me to. It had been such a short amount of time, but so much had happened since the night I let myself mourn my twin. I asked Arro to leave my side for the first time, I needed to know the other spirits were okay, and he knew now that I had the strength to protect myself. No one would hurt again, not without the fight of their lives.

I knew the smaller statues well, but I wanted the largest– the statues that gave the most control. The ones I'd once been too frightened to touch with their spider like cracks and crevices. I approached, walking slowly, my thoughts reaching out as I brushed my fingers against stone after stone.

My thoughts had always been scattered on the other side, infected by people who hurt me. Even now I remembered the depths of the betrayals enacted upon me, but I knew– Cole never betrayed me. I believed in him and he hadn't let me down. He'd gotten angry, sad, or hurt, but he never once hurt me, even when I pushed his limits. I wondered if I'd miss him every day for the rest of my death, but missing him would be worth it, worth every moment of our life together.

As each prayer approached I gave it due time, letting it sink into my bones and letting my visceral response return to them; my love for all of the people I'd never met. The stones were getting larger and larger as I made my way down the path. Until I stood in front of that same guardian with spider veins and cracked pieces peeling falling away. It looked so close to crumbling, but so strong he might stand tall for eternity. My lovely contradiction.

This one. He would show me what I needed to see.

"Cole," I silently called as my fingers brushed the stone.

I could hear his thoughts and wishes. Softly I spoke, "I love you. I'll be waiting for you here, in the world where we can be together. Where we can be anything we want to be. I will always remember you and one day, you will remember me."

I could see the barest shadows of where he must be and saw him turn toward my view. Looking around for the voice that came from nothing.

"I'll be waiting," I whispered.

"Did you hear that?" Cole asked.

"Hear what?" Willow leaned over his shoulder.

"I don't know. It just... I felt..." She met his confusion with a chagrin smile. It looked as though years had passed. "I feel like... ah never mind. It's a silly notion. I just..."

"Cole, trust yourself," she whispered and a tear lay on her eyelashes, stubbornly refusing to fall. She knew. She knew what it was. She could hear me too.

"Take care of him and know you are welcome here. You all are. I won't forget you," I whispered as she walked across the room, away from him, hoping she alone might hear.

"We will never forget you. And know, we may not have known you for long but, Lily, we really do love you. Always. It's like you're here with us still," she whispered under her breath and the ink beneath my skin swirled, painting so much of my life across my skin. I didn't fight. I didn't back down. I was proud of who I had become. Letting my story show, there was no judge here. None that would blame me for the life I led, or the mistakes I'd made.

"Lily? I mean..." Cole asked and I wondered for a moment if he might remember.

"What, my love?" Willow responded to Cole and he shook his head, as though trying to shake off the way the whispers carried my voice.

Give him time, I thought to myself. That's all he needs. He has what you don't and he is using it wisely. I looked around his office, wondering exactly how much time had passed. He looked older, but the only wrinkles gracing his face were caused by joy or worry, not further hardships. Stress creases between his eyebrows were now balanced out by light lines at the edges of his eyes and a crease where his dimples would show as he smiled.

I smiled with them, happy for them. How had so much time passed? And now... I looked at the pictures. He had a daughter. She was the most beautiful child I'd ever seen, even if I was biased. She looked so happy, so carefree. There were so many pictures of her. In each one you could tell she was cherished. I took a closer look and saw the names engraved on one of the frames...

Cole.

Willow.

And...

He still knew me. He remembered me. He named his daughter Lily.

I smiled, knowing that in some strange way fate had given the oddest of gifts. She would live the life I always wanted and while some small part of me couldn't help be jealous, the rest of me was exhilarated. Like a star burning through my heart, the heat so overwhelming. I was a part of something. Something bigger than me.

And somehow that meant everything.

It made everything worthwhile.

I let Cole go and he'd once again proven to be the man I'd always thought. For the first time, I was the one sending out my own silent prayer to whoever might listen. "Keep her safe. Keep her strong. Let her be truly loved and live such a fulfilling life that the stars themselves will be jealous of the way she shines. Let her be everything I didn't have the strength or opportunity to be. Protect her."

The hart of the forest walked out from between two statues and as we watched each other I smiled. He heard me. He whinnied and bucked to his back legs. Rising up so strong and tall that if I hadn't known him to be a part of me, I wouldn't have had the strength to stand tall with him. I felt his confirmation.

She was the child of a shadow of the forest and a man who made a pact out of selflessness. She might know the pain of heartbreak and the emotions any life had to offer, but she would also know love and true joy. This time it would go right. She could have a loving father, the kind anyone would dream of, a mother full of passion and kindness and I'd be here, watching over her from afar.

Until the day we could all be together again.

One day this place could belong to each of us and we could fill it with the beauty none of us could imagine alone. The beauty that any true family– chosen family –brought into the world.

CHAPTER TWENTY TWO

When Arro and I found each other he smiled, seeing the way my demeanor had changed— the aching void in my heart now full. "I understand now."

I wasn't sure how much time passed, seconds or days.

Time no longer held meaning to me. It was simply a vessel to another place.

"Do you really?" he asked, smirking.

My curiosity sparked from the look in his eyes. He sat next to me in the very graveyard I'd first seen the hart in. I'd even manipulated the forest into carving a stone with his name on it— along with Baku's and Koichi's, the water spirit who loved to dance down the falls I would visit whenever I needed a moment to reflect.

"I think so," I responded. "My brother once said that each person has their own world after they die, a world where they can be everything they didn't have the chance to be in life. I think maybe this is mine." It would've sounded farfetched once, but looking at the ever moving violet sky it felt right.

He chuckled darkly. "I guess that makes me your dream guy?"

His smirk made my lips react instinctively, curling into a wide smile as he leaned toward me. "Am I right?" I leaned toward him until our faces were only inches apart.

"In part. It isn't just your world. It's ours. The spirits here build this world. You, as the shadow and voice do too, only more so. With each soul that comes here the beauty grows. It's our world, for the wandering or the lost. A pocket realm, like many others. Why? If you could make this world anything you wanted, what would it be like?"

"I guess mine would be this," I admitted. It was so honest it hurt, but his lips met mine and the pain disappeared. I was lost in him again until he pulled back abruptly.

"Why a forest? I thought you hated them," he asked, holding me by my shoulders to get a good look at me.

"I was always terrified of them. I guess... I wanted to be fearless. I wanted to be brave." I smiled, knowing how much I'd changed.

"Somehow I get the feeling you always were."

It was my turn to steal a kiss from my kitsune.

EPILOGUE

Cole

I walked the line of graves we'd crossed together as children. Passing each one I dropped flowers, as she once had. I even stole them from Ms. Rossum's yard, purely for memory's sake– my own homage to Lily's rebellious nature. Arro Remington... Baku Lloyd... Koichi Sealy... As I stopped in front of Lily's grave I smiled, seeing wild flowers growing there, violet and untamed. They reminded me of a dream from long ago, the strangest dream I'd ever had. I knew I could cut them. Keep her last name showing as proudly as those on the graves around her. Willow visited this graveyard weekly and I knew the other graves were maintained by Sachiko, though I still wasn't quite sure I understood their connection to this place– let alone my sister.

None of us had the heart to kill those strange otherworldly flowers.

The graveyard changed so much through the years.

Everything had, except the now dulled feeling that someone or something was always missing. I knew it was time to say goodbye, but that didn't make it easier. "I hope you finally got a chance to be the one to do the saving. You may not have said it, but I knew... I knew all you ever wanted was to save us both. I hope you swam among the stars and met friends worth keeping. I hope your world was kind to you, like you were always kind to me. It showed who you'd been all along. Lily, you were the most beautiful human being. I wish we could've had adventures there together, but, please, know that you have a legacy.

"I took the pain of losing you and made something new. I help people like you always said I would. I have a daughter named Lisa. Her middle name is Lily and when she found a picture of you, she insisted we call her Lily. Her mother, Willow is the kindest soul you will ever meet. You two would've been kindred spirits. Her father and I run a hospital now. I wish I could have saved you. I'm sorry... I am just so sorry." My hand rose to my chest, clutching the space over my heart before coming down hard on top of the grave I knelt before.

I meant to visit sooner. Seeing the engraving made her death all too real. In my office, with pictures of us and the pictures of my family, I could almost imagine her there with them. Playing with Lisa in the yard or showing her the night sky. I could see her standing there next to us in our family photos. Smiling for the camera when anyone said, "mozzarella" because my girl decided just saying cheese was silly, people should be more specific about things as serious as cheese.

"I tried, Lily, I tried. But no matter how many people I've saved I just couldn't..." My voice went silent as I heard something in the grass next to me.

A fox.

The fox and I watched one another and something about the interaction was familiar to me, even though I knew it to be impossible. My hand reached for my chest and I gasped as my fingers brushed the spot just above my heart.

"I remember you," I whispered softly.

Cole stared as Willow came to his side and knelt before the fox.

It dropped a piece of paper.

"The flowers above my grave are my immortality. Not the ones placed there by loved ones, but the ones that bloom without reason. That small dandelion you just can't seem to get rid of no matter how many times you uproot it. The violet flowers that bloom too quickly and spread too wildly. Don't forget to look at the strange flowers by forgotten graves, for it's there that you'll find what eternity means. It's quite simple really. It means nothing more and nothing less than continuing on. Than...hope. I love you. I love you all so much.

—Lily Rodel"

19865320R00099

Printed in Poland
by Amazon Fulfillment
Poland Sp. z o.o., Wrocław